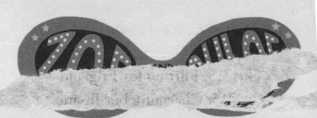

OUT TO
LUNCH

OUT TO
LUNCH

First published in Great Britain in 2008 by Bloomsbury Publishing Plc
36 Soho Square, London, W1D 3QY

A CIP catalogue record of this book is available from the British Library

ISBN 978 0 7475 8273 1

All papers used by Bloomsbury Publishing are natural, recyclable products made
from wood grown in well-managed forests. The manufacturing processes conform
to the environmental regulations of the country of origin.

Typeset by Dorchester Typesetting Group Limited
Printed in Great Britain by Clays Limited, St Ives Plc

1 3 5 7 9 10 8 6 4 2

www.suelimb.co.uk
www.bloomsbury.com

For Amanda Steinson

CHAPTER 1

'What? Four hundred and fifty? Just for a caravan for a week?' Chloe's voice soared upwards in a hysterical shriek. It was the first day of the summer hols, and we were surfing the Newquay websites. We had been dreaming of this holiday for ages, but where were we going to stay? Foolishly, although we'd been fantasising about it for so long, we hadn't got around to arranging any of the practical details.

'We could share with Toby and Fergus . . .' I suggested. 'Between four, it'd only be, uh . . . a hundred and something.'

'*Only?*' wailed Chloe. 'Anyway, we can't share a caravan with Tobe and Ferg. They would, like, see us in our pants and, even worse, we would see them in *their* pants.'

'What sort of pants do you think Ferg wears?' I giggled. Toby and Fergus are our best boy mates at school and, with any luck, we would never get to see their pants for the rest of our entire lives. Tobe's very camp, and Ferg's very tiny, so they're a bit of a comedy duo, but they'd already been a lot more organised than us, getting holiday jobs and saving up loads.

'Ferg's pants . . . ?' Chloe mused. 'Hmmm . . . possibly a pattern of cute yellow mice wearing top hats?'

'Yeah.' I grinned. 'As for Toby, it's got to be pink with lace edges.'

'God, he's so outrageous!' laughed Chloe. 'Isn't it weird how some guys can be camp without being gay?'

'And vice versa,' I mused. 'But, hey! Focus, Chloe! Back to the pressing issue of our accommodation!'

'Chill out! You're such a Victorian governess!' wailed Chloe in mock torment.

'Maybe that explains it all!' I had a moment of revelation. 'Maybe in a previous existence I literally *was* your Victorian governess!'

'Maybe we should get hypnotised and do past-lives regression,' said Chloe eagerly. 'I'm sure I can remember your starchy collar and luxuriant moustache!'

I fingered my upper lip anxiously. The awful thing is, I sometimes think I *really am* getting a moustache. I once spent ten minutes in the bathroom with my dad's shaving mirror and a torch and I detected more than a peachy bloom on my upper lip: it was a *wheat field*. By the time I'm forty I'll need a combine harvester to de-fuzz myself.

'I *know* you were my governess!' giggled Chloe. 'I remember the twang of your corsets! You were still a virgin at sixty-five!'

'Well, you were a crazy Victorian nymphomaniac,' I quipped.

'That is totally unfair!' yelled Chloe hysterically. 'OK, I was a nymphomaniac, but I was so *not* crazy!'

'You had hair two metres long and mad red flashing eyes,' I told her. 'I had to manacle you to the bedpost whenever the footman was passing.'

Chloe giggled and opened a new web page from the Newquay Accommodation website.

'Oh my God!' wailed Chloe. 'Look! It says, *"Our caravans are available to families and over-eighteens only"*!' A huge wave of fatigue swept over me – and I *so* hate huge waves of all sorts.

'Forget it, then,' I said, fingering my chin. There's a spot there called Nigel and he emerges every month along with premenstrual tension. I was feeling tense now. 'Hey, babe – maybe we should leave it till tomorrow.' I had a horrid feeling that the search for accommodation was going to end badly. We'd been feverishly longing for this trip for ages. Everybody at school was going, or said they were: it was practically compulsory to go to Newquay this year.

What if it all went pear-shaped? I slipped into one of my nightmare scenarios. I have them about six times a day.

If we ever got to Newquay, we'd have to sleep on a park bench. No, that would be way too comfy: we'd end up sleeping on the pavement. Dogs would pee on us in the night. Drunks would fall on us. We would be mugged by gangs of feral street-children.

But aside from all this hysterical fantasy stuff, there was a real problem, a huge issue that we'd been kind of ignoring. I think it's called the Elephant in the Room: a really massive thing that nobody dares mention. I knew I was going to have to be the one to broach the subject.

'Hey, wait a min!' said Chloe, still ripping through endless Newquay web pages. 'What about hostels?' She typed *Newquay hostels* into Google. 'Wow!' she breathed. 'This looks great! It says it's the fave place

10

for surfers! And they don't have a curfew! We could pull a couple of heavenly boys and sit out on the beach with them, all night.'

'If we're going to sit out on the beach with heavenly boys all night,' I grinned, 'why bother with a hostel at all?' Somehow, in my imagination, one of the heavenly boys was faintly familiar: tall and dark and mysterious-looking. I picked up a pen and idly wrote the name Oliver on my arm like a kind of tattoo.

'We could live on the beach!' yelled Chloe in excitement. 'We could build ourselves a house of sand! We could become mermaids!' Then, suddenly, everything changed. 'Oh, no!' Her fingers came to a halt, and all the excitement died in her voice. 'How totally unfair!'

'What?' I asked, full of dread. I was already convinced that nobody in the whole of Newquay would accept two under-eighteens on their own. We'd have to disguise ourselves as our own grandmothers.

'*They* don't accept anybody under eighteen, either,' growled Chloe. 'Tight or what? An Eighteen-and-Over hostel!'

'What kind of lifestyle do they have in these hostels?' I shook my head in disbelief. 'A life of rampant sex and violence?'

'Pornographic breakfasts?' suggested Chloe, getting into it. 'Two fried eggs and a sausage?'

'Served by gothic wenches in bondage gear?' I added. 'A severed head on the mantelpiece – of a guest who hasn't paid his bill?'

'En suite torture chambers!' giggled Chloe. 'Oh look!' She was still racing through the web pages at the speed of light. 'This one says, "*Guests aged between sixteen and eighteen will be accepted only if accompanied by a letter of consent from their parents*"!'

Chloe turned to me, alarm flickering in her green eyes. This was the Elephant in the Room: we hadn't told our parents.

'We're going to have to tell them some time,' I said. 'Why not now?'

Right on cue, we heard Chloe's mum's key in the lock.

CHAPTER 2

Chloe went pale. Her mum, Fran, is totally lovely, an old hippie who believes in peace and love and the tarot. She works in a shop where they sell wind chimes and organic cereal and stuff. But all the same, Chloe went pale. Neither of us had been on a holiday by ourselves before, not counting the horrendous school trip to Gorget-St-Marie, where Chloe's French pen pal forgot to show her where the loo was (outside – in a shed covered with ivy).

But Chloe's French loo crisis was nothing compared to what was looming now.

'Let's tell your mum!' I whispered. 'Get her on our side! Then she can help to persuade my mum!' My mum was going to be an even bigger challenge.

'Don't say anything!' hissed Chloe. 'Leave it to

me! It depends on her mood!'

A large dog shot into the room and jumped into Chloe's arms. She staggered backwards. I've sometimes thought Chloe's dog, Geraint, could be a dress rehearsal for a certain sort of boyfriend. A pervy one. He once did something quite unrepeatable to my mum's leg – and I don't mean weeing on it, either. Being weed on would be a picnic compared to what Geraint did.

'Hi, darlings!' called Fran. She bustled in, carrying a basket full of some kind of green leafy vegetable. She was wearing a skirt covered with mirrors, a gilet embroidered with red camels, and earrings the shape of small tigers. A powerful pong of jasmine had entered the room with her. Just looking at her was like going on a trip to India without having to endure a long-haul flight. 'You haven't been sitting at that wretched computer all day, I hope!' cried Fran.

'No! No!' insisted Chloe, scrambling off the computer chair and joining her mum in the kitchen. She gave her a hug. 'We've been looking for work.'

'Of course you ought to spend some of the hols earning money if you can,' said Fran, swiftly unpacking her shopping bag and putting the kettle on. 'But really, I hope you'll find time to relax as well.'

'We are!' I blurted. 'We're going to . . .'

'We're going to chill out in the park every afternoon!' Chloe interrupted me with a warning glare. It was her job to tell her mum about Newquay, not mine, so I reluctantly bit my lip.

'Oh, the park, how lovely!' said Fran. 'Just make me a cup of tea, would you, Chloe? I'm going to be late for my yoga . . .' She ran upstairs to change.

'You missed the perfect opportunity, then!' I whispered. 'It was handed to us on a plate!'

'She's stressed out!' hissed Chloe. 'It's the wrong moment! She could go ballistic just like that!' I've never seen Fran go ballistic, and really, compared with my mum's tantrums, I was sure it would be a storm in a teacup. When my mum goes ballistic, the sky goes black, the oceans boil, and mountains in South America rumble ominously.

'Let's soften her up by telling her all about the job we're going to get!' I suggested. There was the sound of the shower being turned on upstairs.

'Quick! Quick! Let's find some jobs on the Internet!' Chloe raced back to the PC. 'We should have done that before looking for the accommodation in Newquay! We're such morons!'

We found an employment agency-type website

15

which began with a form to fill in. '*REGISTER TODAY*,' it demanded. Chloe raced through this. The password we chose was YAUQWEN – Newquay backwards. It sounded like the ancient Aztec god of unhappy cats.

Once the registration was completed, we moved to the next stage of the form. It said, '*Please choose four sectors in which you have experience or qualifications.*' Then there was a long list of horrid things, including words like Logistics and Defence and Management and Executive.

'It says Media!' cried Chloe. 'Let's choose that!' Evidently she was hoping to get a holiday job directing films or something.

'We can't choose that!' I giggled. 'We haven't got either experience or qualifications in Media, you muppet! In fact we haven't got experience or qualifications in any of these sectors. This website is for adults who are already launched in their careers! It's a non-starter!'

'Yeah,' Chloe agreed. 'We're totally wasting our time here.'

'Let's ring the supermarkets and ask if they've got any work,' I suggested. 'I saw Fred Parsons working in the fish department last Sunday – wearing a stylish white trilby hat and flanked by a pair of gorgeous pouting haddocks.'

'Now that's what I call a lifestyle!' grinned Chloe. 'You ring them. You know I'm useless on the phone. Tell them we're friends of Fred's. Tell them I want to work in Cheese.'

'Why do I always have to do the phoning?' I grumbled, heading for the phone. 'I reckon you've got a phone phobia or something.' I grabbed the Yellow Pages.

'Well, you've got a phobia about slugs,' Chloe pointed out. 'And if you give me any more lip I'm gonna drop a couple of biggies down the back of your dress!'

I did a sort of screaming laugh and grabbed the phone. While Chloe made us a cup of spiced chai (our favourite tipple – kind of milky tea with cinnamon) and some ordinary tea for her mum, I rang all three of the local supermarkets and discovered that all the holiday jobs for people our age had been filled way back at Easter or something. There were no vacancies 'at this late stage' as one woman put it. Chloe and I had clearly failed to grasp the most basic principles of getting a job: be there at dawn, three months early.

There was a local paper on one of the kitchen worktops: smeared with ketchup but still readable. I grabbed it and looked for the Jobs section. Then I read out a few extracts in a silly posh voice. ' "*Do you have sufficient breadth of experience to be our Hydrogen Product Manager?*" '

'We must have some experience of hydrogen,' said Chloe. 'It's a gas, right?'

'Passing swiftly on,' I continued, ' "*Early morning cleaners required for retail store.*" '

'Early morning?' cried Chloe in alarm. 'Oh no! It's bad enough having to get up early to go to school. Let's find a nice afternoon job so we can have some lovely lie-ins.'

' "*Brightwell House Nursery: part-time staff . . .*" '

'No! I can't cope with little kids! They scare me!' I share Chloe's fear and loathing of small children. In fact, I've babysat for the toddlers from hell – the Norman twins. Call me prejudiced if you like, but I do prefer to spend quality time with people who won't pee over me from a great height or wake me up by thrashing me with a rubber snake – two of the *least* offensive things the Norman twins have done. If I ever have children they're going to have to be born as teenagers.

At this point we heard Fran coming downstairs.

'Go for it!' I hissed. Chloe shook her head and flapped her hands, about to indicate that if I were to be so rash as to mention Newquay, she would have a terrible revenge, possibly involving slugs or even – more horrifying still – small children.

Fran's yoga kit consists of wide-legged trousers in a tropical print and a kind of canvas tent top with sleeves. The tiger earrings had been replaced with a couple of pine trees – presumably because they were more yogic than tigers.

'I'm late! I'm late! Where's that tea? Oh, bless you!' Fran stood and slurped her tea.

'We were thinking of getting a job for a month or so,' I said.

'Good idea!' said Fran, looking as if she was hoping I wouldn't say anything else. 'Brilliant! Try that employment agency in the high street.'

'We're going there in a minute,' I lied. 'And if we do find a job, we're going to follow your advice . . .' (this was cunning) 'and leave the last week of the hols free to relax and chill out in New . . .' Chloe kicked me, 'in new chic ways,' I concluded.

'Great! Wonderful! Where's my bag? I must go – see you later!'

And she whirled out with a slam of the door and a *tinkle, tinkle* of the wind chimes in the hall (supplied at a discount by her shop).

'Zoe! How dare you nearly mention Newquay when I'd specifically told you not to!' snapped Chloe. 'It was so the wrong moment. You must let me ask her in my own time! My mum can be unexpectedly weird about stuff – she still hasn't given me my sex talk yet!'

'You're the lucky one.' I grinned. 'My mum gave me my first sex talk when I was five, and I've had to sit through one every year since. Anyway, once Fran knows we're heading for Newquay I think you'll find the sex talk will swiftly follow.'

'I hope it never comes!' shrieked Chloe. 'I couldn't bear the thought of my mum even using the words!'

'It would be better if the words were different,' I pondered. 'How about: the man puts his blancmange into the woman's apple crumble?'

'No! Not food! Food is gross!' screeched Chloe, placing our mugs of chai on a tin tray decorated with the god Vishnu. 'How about: the man puts his Piccadilly into the woman's Swindon?'

'Or animals? The man puts his aardvark into the woman's Chihuahua?' Laughing helplessly we carried the tray out into Chloe's back garden. It's like a cute little fragment of rainforest. Her mum has carved out a kind of arbour among the trees, and installed some garden furniture. It's old garden furniture, obviously. Fran's idea of chic is decidedly shabby.

I placed the tray on the rickety old table and plonked myself down in one of the ancient wicker chairs. There was a ripping sound of old sticks giving way as my arse tore straight through the chair seat and went on plummeting towards the earth twenty-five centimetres below.

'Jesus!' I yelled as my bot struck terra firma. Chloe cracked up. She laughed so much, she half fell on to the rickety table and spilled most of the chai. I struggled to my feet, but the wicker chair was kind of fastened round my bum like a cartoon out of *The Dandy*. 'Pull it off! Pull it off!' I gasped, hysterical. Eventually Chloe stopped weeping with laughter and held on to the chair while I tugged myself out of it.

'If only we'd videoed that!' said Chloe, groaning at the comic perfection of the moment. 'We could have used it as a show reel and got jobs as TV comedians!'

Once we'd got the chair off my bum, the laughter died. The chair looked terrible: kind of sad and trashed. It had been a dear old chair and I was sure it was Fran's favourite. Maybe it could be mended by a lovable old guy with a silvery moustache, a leather apron and a willow plantation behind his cute thatched cottage.

We had to find that man, even though the bill for repairs would probably cost more than a week in Newquay. The need for cash was more urgent than ever.

'Look,' I said, 'let's go to that employment office your mum mentioned. You know, just up from the station. What's it called? – Mercury. At least let's just go there in person and ask. It can't do any harm.'

CHAPTER 3

The trip to Mercury Employment involved a short bus journey and we got off just by the Dolphin Cafe. I suddenly remembered that Toby had a holiday job there. He is way more organised than we are. I think he applied for the job back in April or something. We went in and found a table.

Moments later Toby came mincing out of the kitchen carrying a tray with four steaming mugs of tea. When he saw us he kind of twitched, and I was scared, for a mo, that he might drop the tray or even hurl it all over the customers, causing a lawsuit – and, obviously, Toby would get the sack and it would all be my fault. My mum's in insurance and sometimes I think I've inherited her 'disaster scenario' way of thinking.

We giggled secretly as we watched Tobe serve the family with their tea. He was terrifically polite and gracious, but his waiter's trousers were just slightly stuck up his crack. Then he came across to us.

'Good afternoon, ladies!' he pouted. 'How may I help you?'

'God, Toby, you so look the part!' giggled Chloe. 'That long apron and stuff!'

'So Parisian!' I agreed.

'Any vacancies here?' asked Chloe. 'We're disastrously unemployed.'

'We're such retards,' I wailed. 'If we can't find work, our fabulous hol in Newquay is going down the pan!' Tobe went pale.

'You can't chicken out now!' he hissed. 'We've been planning it since we were embryos!'

'Well, get us a job here, then!' demanded Chloe.

'No chance,' whispered Toby. 'Maria only employs boys, for reasons which must remain private. So! Can I take your order?'

'Oh, definitely!' I agreed. 'I'd like a cranberry pressé, please, waiter.'

'And could I get an elderflower pressé?' asked Chloe. The Dolphin Cafe has gone a bit upmarket since Maria took it over in May. She used to be just the waitress and she's famously the worst flirt in town, but with stunning business sense, obviously.

'How's it going here, anyway?' I asked.

'Oh, great!' Toby grinned. 'Maria says I can be her toy boy on Thursdays!'

'Why only Thursdays?' asked Chloe.

'There's a rota!' whispered Toby – then he bounced off back to the kitchen.

'Shame Ferg couldn't work here as well,' I commented. 'He could protect Toby from Maria.' Fergus was working in his dad's warehouse, though it was hard to imagine tiny Ferg heaving cardboard boxes about. However, Ferg was earning big time – though he's small, his bank balance is often bigger than anybody's, and he's so organised and motivated, he writes down every financial transaction in a little notebook – even his chewing-gum purchases.

After finishing our drinks we set off towards the employment agency with renewed urgency.

'We've just *got* to find work,' I said anxiously. 'We just have to! If there's nothing at the employment agency I think we should go round all the shops asking if they want extra help, OK?'

'God, yes!' said Chloe. 'We so *have* to get to Newquay! Think of the sun – the surf – the surfers –

oh, it'll be brilliant! Nothing's gonna stand in our way.'

Arm in arm we strode towards Mercury Employment. We could not have been more committed. Then, with a sudden lurch of alarm, I saw him.

It was too late to protect Chloe from a really awkward meeting. He was coming towards us, only about a hundred metres away. He'd had a haircut, so his long greasy locks had gone, which is probably why I hadn't recognised him in time. If I had, I'd have steered Chloe into the nearest shop, grabbed a random dress or two and hidden in the changing room.

'Oh my God!' hissed Chloe. 'It's Beast!'

'Just walk past,' I said. 'Keep talking. Ignore him.' Chloe gripped my arm tightly. I had to get her past him in one piece. After all, he had broken her heart quite recently, and behaved like an utter cad.

'Hey! Zoe and Chloe!' He hailed us from some distance. 'My favourite double act!'

'Let's run!' whispered Chloe.

'No way!' I commanded. 'We just act totally normal. Leave it to me.' There are times when I have to switch into Frightening Victorian Governess mode and protect Chloe, because despite all her fun and fizz and recklessness, she can seem really fragile and I can't bear it when people hurt her.

'How's it goin', girls?' he said, grinning, with his usual cocksure flirtatiousness. 'You're both looking amazing as usual. So what's new?'

Chloe's grip tightened. Her fingernails were now almost through my skin. 'We're great,' she said. 'How are you?'

'Oh, fine, you know. Busy.' He grinned, looking down at Chloe with that awful glamorous gaze which had so easily paralysed her in the past. And then he turned it on me. I just stared back, bold as brass.

'Where's your handsome sidekick?' I enquired sarcastically. Beast's usual companion is a boy called Donut, who resembles a giant root vegetable.

'Oh, Donut's gone to Kenya,' said Beast. 'Some kind of safari thing.'

'Why didn't you go with him?' I asked, implying Beast was a wimp for staying at home while his turnip-faced buddy wrestled with lions or possibly learnt to cuss in Swahili.

'Oh, I've got to stay here,' said Beast. 'I've got a job with an events and hospitality company. What are you up to?'

'We're going to be working for about a month,' said Chloe.

'And then we're going to Newquay for a week,' I added.

'Newquay?' exclaimed Beast. 'Awesome! See you there! Me and the guys from the rugby team are going to be there in the last week of August. I'll teach you to surf if you like.'

'We're not really completely and utterly sure if we're going to Newquay yet,' I countered, panicking. I didn't want Beast pushing his brawny way into Chloe's poor battered little heart again. 'Flora Barclay's invited us to join her in Tuscany – you never know . . .' Chloe gave me an astonished look. 'Plus we've been thinking about Brighton – my aunt lives there,' I said, inventing an aunt on the spot. I had always wanted an aunt in Brighton. I was fond of her already. Especially if she was going to rescue us from the clutches of Beast.

'Is that right?' enquired Beast. He twinkled his eyes at us, trying to soften us up, but I gritted my teeth and looked as grim as possible. 'Brighton's cool,' he went on, 'but the beach is crap compared to Cornwall, and the surf is nil. So where are you going to be working, then?'

'We haven't actually found a job yet,' said Chloe.

'So we'd better get our skates on,' I added, starting to move away. 'We've gotta go. We've got an appointment and we're going to be late for it. Come on, Chloe,' I said, and stepped out. I still had her arm firmly entwined in mine, so she could hardly resist without breaking her shoulder.

'See you around, then!' Beast grinned. We marched firmly away. Chloe gave a stifled little sound of pain, like a sob or a gasp.

'Don't cry!' I demanded. 'He's not worth it!'

'I'm not going to cry!' snapped Chloe. 'Just let me go, for God's sake! You're breaking my freakin' arm!'

I released my grip. 'Sorry!' I muttered. 'I just can't stand that guy. He makes me sick. Everything about him makes my skin creep. Think about the horrible way he treated you!'

'Don't be so melodramatic!' Chloe exclaimed. 'It's no big deal.'

'But you wanted to run away just now,' I pointed out.

'I want to run away from loads of people,' snapped Chloe. 'It doesn't mean I'm mad about them!'

I didn't believe her. I could see it all so clearly: we'd be down in Newquay, and Chloe would bump into Beast, and he'd start his charming seductive act all over again, and he'd be telling her how beautiful she was and stuff, just like before . . .

And then he'd dump her, just like that, out of the blue, because some gorgeous girl had come along, and Chloe would go mental, and spend all day crying, and throw herself in the sea, and be eaten by killer whales, and instead of sending her mum, Fran, a postcard, I'd be presenting her with a horrid little shoebox, in which would be all that was left of Chloe.

'Maybe we shouldn't go to Newquay after all,' I suggested doubtfully. 'I mean, there are other places.'

'What?' gasped Chloe, stopping stock-still and grabbing my sleeve.

'You could completely lose it if Beast was there,' I said.

'I so would *not*! Don't be stupid!'

'We can go somewhere else,' I said. 'Another surfing place.'

'Well, I'm going to Newquay, even if you aren't!' shouted Chloe. 'How can you be such an idiot? You've just no idea what you're talking about!'

'I'm only thinking of you,' I insisted.

'Well, freakin' well stop thinking of me, Zoe!' Chloe's eyes flared and her face went bright red. 'Get outta my face!' And she turned on her heel and stomped off back in the direction we'd come – the direction, of course, where Beast had so recently disappeared. I didn't argue. I just kind of slumped.

I wandered along, staring at the pavement for a bit. What else could I do? Just five minutes ago we'd been determined to get a job right now, starting in half an hour if possible, then Beast had disastrously arrived and it had all gone pear-shaped. Chloe and I had wasted our time yelling at each other and now I'd totally lost my drive and motivation.

I was so distracted by our row and by Beast's inconvenient reappearance, I was kind of unaware of my surroundings. Suddenly a pair of black shoes appeared in front of me.

'Hello,' said a voice.

CHAPTER 4

I looked up. It was Oliver! Oliver Wyatt! I hadn't seen him for weeks, but I'd thought of him about every three minutes. Only an hour or so ago I'd written his name on my arm. Hastily I pulled down the sleeve of my cardi.

Oliver looked simply magnificent. Every drop of blood in my body flew to my face, causing my spot, Nigel, to throb like some kind of disco strobe light. Bongo drums throbbed in my neck. A tsunami of spit surged up my throat, causing me to cough and choke. I tried to look casual, well-dressed and mildly pleased to see him, but biology was against me.

He, of course, looked fabulous. Pale, tall, more Mr Darcyish than ever in his white open-necked shirt. A lock of hair fell across his brow. Would I ever get to stroke that brow? Would I ever run my fingers through those dark locks? I tried to look serious and cool, but I knew I looked farcical and sweaty.

'Oliver!' I said, as if I'd almost forgotten who he was, forgotten his name, even though I've written it on my hand a hundred times. 'Hey! How's it going?'

'Yeah, cool, fine,' he said.

There was a silence, during which perspiration broke out on my upper lip with a resounding splash.

'I just met Beast Hawkins,' I said. 'He's organising events or something. What are you doing this summer?'

'I'm working on a farm,' said Oliver.

'Oh yeah!' I blushed. 'I remember you were looking for a job on a farm.' I'd been hoping to forget that awful little episode, when I'd once impulsively pretended to live on a farm so as to impress Oliver, then it all spiralled out of control when he actually rang my dad and asked for work mucking out the pigs. 'What's it like?'

'Amazing, yeah,' said Oliver. 'I've only been there a fortnight but, well . . . it's good.'

'I wish I could work on a farm!' I sighed. 'Chloe and I are actually looking for work right now.'

'Are you?' Oliver looked faintly interested. 'I think

they're looking for extra labour at the place where I'm working. In the veg fields.' My heart gave a gigantic leap, kind of head-butting me in the tonsils.

'Really?' I gasped. 'Are you sure . . . ?'

'Yeah,' he said. 'Martin – he's the farmer – was talking about it yesterday. Why don't you give him a ring and ask about it? Tell him I mentioned it.'

He got out a little diary and wrote Martin's number on one of the pages. His fingers were beautiful and long and I could see his handwriting was kind of crazy and slanting. I wondered what it was like holding hands with him, and whether his were cool or warm. He tore out the page and handed it to me.

'Fantastic!' I gushed. 'Thanks so much! So, might see you there, then?' I tried to look casual, but I knew I resembled a breathless little dog that has been promised walkies. I was practically wagging my tail and panting.

'Yeah!' Oliver nodded, shrugged and backed away slightly awkwardly – a sign that he was about to say goodbye. But he couldn't totally hate me and want to say goodbye to me for ever, could he? Or he wouldn't have encouraged me to get a job at the farm! My heart was hammering away like mad. If I got really lucky, I could be working with Oliver every day for the next four weeks! How amazing would that be?

'Bye!' I grinned, looking up at him. Suddenly I noticed a tiny bogey at the corner of his right nostril. It wasn't gross. It was kind of charming. I would have killed for that bogey. I would have kept it in a matchbox and called it Charlie.

'OK, then – bye,' said Oliver. He gave me a shy sideways little smile, moved a step or two away, and did a weird stiff little wave. I replied with a preposterous kind of toss of the head, which was supposed to look casual and stylish, but actually jarred my brain and hurt quite a lot. He backed off into a lamp-post. We both laughed slightly as if it was no big deal. And then he turned away and walked off. It seemed to have taken ten years to say goodbye.

It wasn't horrid, parting with him, though, because of the wonderful opportunities that had opened up. I abandoned all my previous plans. To hell with Mercury Employment! I was going to work with Oliver!

I got out my moby and rang the farm right away. The line wasn't brilliant, and there were some dogs barking in the background, but two minutes later it was all sorted – I'd fixed up a month's work for

Chloe and me at Old Hall Farm, Sheepscombe-on-Stour, a short bus ride from town, at £3.50 an hour, the standard rate for people our age – 'Take it or leave it,' Martin had said in a rather challenging way.

I assured him £3.50 an hour would be dandy. I'd have *paid* twice that to work in the same place as Oliver Wyatt. I walked to the bus stop in a delirious haze. Now all I had to do was break the wonderful news to Chloe and my family.

On the bus on the way home I tried to ring Chloe on her mobile and her landline, but they were both on voicemail. Never mind – when I got home, at least I'd be able to soak up the praise of my mum and dad, and my glamorous sister, Tamsin, would have to relinquish her starring role for a split second.

But as I walked up my front path I could clearly hear the sound of screaming within.

'It's all arranged!' That was my mum – steely and rigid, but with the volume turned up. 'What *is* this? What in the world do you *mean*?'

'You never asked me!' That, in a kind of wail, was my big sister, Tam.

'We discussed it over and over! You were all for it a fortnight ago!'

'I can't help it! I don't feel very well! You wouldn't want to go to Granny's if you weren't feeling very well!'

I opened the front door and went in. They were in the sitting room. I decided to avoid the row and go straight upstairs.

'Zoe!' Mum called. 'Come in here a minute!'

'Leave me out of this,' I said, standing in the doorway. 'They can hear you shouting in Africa!'

Mum was wearing her business suit. She's always a bit more imposing when she's in her work togs. She's an insurance broker or something. I've never completely understood insurance, and I'm not sure I want to.

'Look,' I said, trying to soothe the frayed nerves, 'why don't I go and make us a cup of tea? I hate rows.' I glanced at Tam, but she avoided eye contact and ducked through the patio doors out into the garden. I wondered what the problem was. There had been a plan for her to go and spend a few days with Granny down in Somerset. Tam adores Granny and would normally be off like a shot. I hoped she wasn't really ill. A lot of people at uni had had glandular fever, including her best mate, Parvati. Oh God! Was it infectious?

'A cup of tea would be a lovely idea, thanks, darling,' said Mum abruptly, collapsing into her favourite large armchair and kicking off her cruel businesswoman's shoes. She was obviously pretty stressed out. Just an average day for Mum involves interviewing people whose houses have burned down and stuff. And here was Tam getting up her nose for some reason.

I went into the kitchen and put the kettle on. Then I opened the back door and stepped out into the garden. Tam was hiding at the far end, by the shed, smoking a cigarette.

'Oh no!' I groaned. 'You're not smoking again, Tam!'

'It's only because I'm so pissed off,' said Tam. 'Anyway, it's just a pack of ten. Stop being such a puritan.'

'Look,' I whispered, 'what's wrong? You were looking forward to going to Granny's. What's happened?'

Tam glanced furtively in the direction of the patio doors. Mum was safely in the sitting room. The sound of the TV broke out: the news. Mum's little addiction.

'I met somebody,' said Tam quietly. 'A couple of

days ago at a cricket match. It's been amazing. He's called Ed. He's amazing. It's all just totally amazing.'

One of the things I hate about love is that it really limits your vocabulary. Also, it makes a fool of you. Tam was staring dreamy-eyed at the garden shed, as if Ed might possibly be hidden inside, folded away behind the door and waiting to come out at night and be amazing in the moonlight.

'He's a photographer,' she said. 'Not professionally, but he's brilliant. He specialises in landscapes, but he took reels and reels of moody black-and-white photos of me. They're just amazing. And he kept saying these ridiculous things . . .'

'So he's *amazing* and it's all *amazing*,' I said, 'and presumably you're in lurrve and he thinks you're the most beautiful creature on God's earth . . . so what's the problem?'

'I can't go to Granny's now!' wailed Tam softly. 'I couldn't bear it! We've only just –'

'Don't tell me what you've only just done,' I begged.

'We've only just *realised* . . .' said Tam, her eyes huge with love drama. Tam had a completely marvellous life, but she still had to behave as though everything that happened was a cruel disaster.

Sometimes I think she's a tiny bit spoilt – but then she turns the tables and spoils me, so it's all very confusing.

I heard the kettle switch itself off in the kitchen, and went back indoors. Tam followed me wanly. I made a pot of Earl Grey and got some of Prince Charles's classy biscuits out for Mum. She's such a snob, biscuit-wise: she won't eat anything unless it was made by a man with a title.

'Going to see Granny was all Mum's idea,' hissed Tam, picking savagely at a loaf of bread and eating chunks of it. 'She fixed it all up. I just went along with it. Listen – I'm going to stage an illness, sometime in the next day or two, and I want you to back me up, OK? It'll have to revolve around pains, because you can't test for pains. And exhaustion. I'm going upstairs to look illnesses up on the Internet. Come up in a min and give me a hand, OK?'

I carried the tea tray in to Mum, who had fallen asleep in front of the news. She woke up with a sudden start. I poured the tea.

'Oh dear, not ordinary tea, I was hoping for Earl Grey,' she said – still fixated on noble and royal catering. 'Never mind, it doesn't matter.'

'It *is* Earl Grey!' I snapped. I had been hoping

for gratitude but it seemed that was not currently available. Halfway through pouring the tea, I was distracted by my mobile ringing. It was Chloe.

'Great news,' she said. 'It's all sorted! I've got us a wonderful job for a month and it's £4.20 an hour!'

CHAPTER 5

I rushed out into the garden, panicking on all cylinders. 'No, listen!' I hissed, '*I've* got us a job!' I thought I'd mention the rate of pay later because it was a side issue.

'But I've already told them we'll start on Monday!'

'Well, I've told *my* job we can start on Monday and my job is way more exciting than any other job could be!'

'What's so damn exciting about it?' demanded Chloe.

'It's on a farm!' I told her. 'The same farm where Oliver Wyatt is working! In fact, he fixed it up for us!'

'A farm?' yelled Chloe. 'No way! I'm frightened of cattle! It'll be mank and smelly with piles of poo

42

everywhere! My job is way more stylish and fun!'

'What's your job, then?' I asked impatiently. I was so fixated on working on Oliver's farm I couldn't really care less about Chloe's precious job, but I kind of had to ask.

'It's with that events company that Beast is working for,' said Chloe. 'Organising weddings and parties and catering and stuff. He says they need an extra two staff and we'll spend the summer in a haze of continuous parties!'

'I might have known you'd go running off to Beast!' I sighed.

'I so did *not* go running off to him!' shouted Chloe. 'I happened to bump into him in the street again, just after I left you, and we went for a coffee.'

'Oh, well, if you're determined to let him break your heart all over again . . .'

'I *so* am not!' snapped Chloe. 'I am totally over Beast, OK? I swear to you on the sacred name of Orlando Bloom that I am completely and utterly over him.'

'Well, in that case,' I said, 'I'm glad and stuff, obviously, but I am so *not* over Oliver, and my job is a chance for me to see him, like, every day and really get to know him.' There was a brief silence.

'How much does your job pay?' demanded Chloe.

'About the same as yours,' I lied recklessly.

'What would we be doing?'

'Working in lovely fields and stuff.' I was busking it a bit, now. 'I think Oliver said something about the veg fields.'

'I hate veg,' said Chloe grumpily.

'You don't have to eat them, Chloe,' I said. 'Only, well, harvest them, maybe. Or feed them and water them and exercise them or something.' I may have been thinking of horses – I'm so inexperienced, I've never ridden fifty metres on a horse, let alone a turnip.

'What do we have to wear?' asked Chloe crossly. 'Horrible cagoules and stuff, I suppose.'

'No – only lovely T-shirts and shorts and things.' I was trying to make the job sound like a holiday. 'We could get a tan.'

'Zoe! I burn to a crisp in the sun! You're talking serious health risks!'

'A hat and some sunscreen!' I blustered. 'Long-sleeved shirts! We won't be working outdoors all the time anyway! Some of the time we'll be in a lovely cool barn!' I was winging it, here, in desperation.

'And what would we be doing in this lovely cool barn?' asked Chloe in a sarcastic voice.

'We'd be looking after baby lambs,' I assured her. 'With their cute big eyes and their fluff and their clip-clop little hooves.' There was a long silence.

'OK,' said Chloe with a massive martyred sigh. 'Beast's job was going to be loads of fun – they're doing a party on a river boat next week for a start – but if you'd rather wallow in piles of dung that's up to you.' Then her voice changed, softening slightly. She heaved another huge sigh. 'I realise that what with Oliver working there, it's too big a deal for you to miss.'

'Oh, Chloe!' I gushed. 'You're a star! Thanks so much! I'm sorry I was on your case about Beast! I'll never mention him again.'

'OK,' said Chloe briskly. 'He's going to be really gutted, but never mind. How do we get there? Where is this joint?'

'Sheepscombe-on-Stour.'

'Sheepscombe-on-Stour? Sounds like a sandwich!' Chloe quipped acidly. I laughed long and loud to encourage her in this new sportive mood.

'The number forty-six bus goes right there,' I said, having got these details from Martin. 'And Old Hall Farm is only a half-mile walk from the bus stop.'

'So high heels are out, then,' Chloe commented

archly. She doesn't often wear high heels anyway these days – not since she fell off her wedges and sprained her ankle at a gig.

'So see you at the bus station at 8.15 on Monday morning,' I said excitedly. 'Thanks so much for going along with this, Chloe. I owe you big time and I won't forget it.'

After I'd rung off, I just stood in the garden for a moment and took some deep breaths. Thank God Chloe had been so generous about it, so totally, unexpectedly nice. She was a star. Now I could go and tell Mum all about the fabulous job I'd fixed up, and maybe she'd be impressed for once.

Suddenly Tam appeared, fumbling with her cigarette packet again. 'Ed just sent me an amazing text,' she said. 'It was a poem. Amazing!'

'Let's see it, then.' I held out my hand. Anything for a laugh. Tam looked embarrassed and hid her moby in her sleeve.

'Er – it's a bit personal,' she said. 'God, Zoe, I wish you could meet him! He's kind of tall, well, taller than Dad, about six foot two I should think, and he's got this amazing hair . . .'

'Hair!? I'm amazed.' I grinned, but she wasn't even listening.

'It's, well, fair,' said Tam, 'but not ordinary fair. It's halfway between straw and – uh . . .'

'Grass?' I enquired. 'Tobacco?'

'Tobacco, yes, exactly!' said Tam. She hadn't realised I was taking the piss. 'His eyes are brown, too, kind of hazel. So unusual!'

'Amazing,' I commented.

'Yes, he looks kind of old-fashioned. Like an Elizabethan lord in an old oil painting!'

'What about his nose?' I enquired. 'Is that also like the amazing nose of a lord in an oil painting?'

'To be honest,' Tam was so focused on describing her beloved that she was totally oblivious to my sarcastic asides, 'his nose is a bit small, for a man. It's kind of cute and turned up. If we had a daughter . . .' She went off into a thrilling fantasy for a moment. I stared at some stones to pass the time. 'If she inherited his nose, that would be perfect.'

'Although she might inherit Grandpa's nose,' I said, 'which, let's face it, is more like an elephant's trunk.' Tam wasn't listening. She was lighting another cigarette.

'What does Ed think of you smoking?' I asked sharply. She looked up defiantly.

'Oh, Ed smokes,' she said airily with a toss of the

head. 'He hates all this politically correct crap.'

'It's not *politically correct* not to smoke,' I explained slowly, as if to a foreign child. 'Smoking kills. It says so on the packet.'

'Oh, shut up, Zoe! Stop preaching all the time!' snarled Tam. I decided to leave her to her foul habits and turned back towards the house. 'Wait! Zoe!' Tam clutched at my sleeve. 'I'm sorry.' She peered at me earnestly. 'I'm in a bit of a state. How are you?'

'I'm fine,' I said. 'In fact, I've just found a job on a farm for me and Chloe, so we can earn enough money to pay for our hol in Newquay. But don't mention Newquay to Mum, because I haven't actually had a chance to run it past the parents yet.'

'Amazing, amazing,' sighed Tam dreamily. 'Working on a farm . . .' I could tell she was fantasising about herself and Ed pulling turnips or possibly rolling in the hay. She linked her arm through mine and chucked her cigarette into the flower beds.

'Do I smell of smoke?' she whispered as we neared the patio doors.

'You smell like the Great Fire of London,' I said.

'Mum will kill me if she finds out I'm smoking again,' said Tam. 'Now listen,' she went on in a whisper, 'on Monday I'm going to stage a collapse, so

I don't have to go to Granny's – I want you to back me up, yeah?'

We entered the sitting room. Mum was sipping her tea and watching yet more depressing news.

'Have you come to your senses yet?' Mum asked Tam. I saw Tam bristle. But she controlled her impulse to throw things.

'OK, Mum, sorry – yeah, I'll go to Granny's, fine – I just need to reschedule a few things . . . But never mind about that – guess what!' She skilfully changed the subject. 'Zoe's got a summer job on a farm!'

Mum's face broke out in sunny smiles. She patted the sofa beside her. 'Well done, darling!' She beamed. 'Come and tell me all about it!'

'Isn't it great?' Tam went on. I knew her game. The more Mum was pleased with me, the less cross she would be about Tam. 'Now Zoe will be able to save up enough for her amazing holiday in Newquay!' announced Tam with a dazzling smile.

My heart lurched in horror. That idiot Tam! She had totally forgotten my warning about not mentioning Newquay! Maybe she hadn't even heard it! She'd been dreaming about Ed! If I ever met him, I would kill him. I'd kill him *twice*.

The sunlight faded from Mum's face and an

ominous cloud gathered between her brows.

'What holiday in Newquay?' she glared. 'This is news to me.'

'Well, it's almost news to me too,' I said, lying through my teeth. Chloe and I had been dreaming about Newquay for months. 'We only cooked up the idea yesterday.' I had to fight hard to refrain from glaring at Tam. I would kick her later – in stereo, with both legs at once. I would grow an extra leg to kick her threefold. But right now I had to convince Mum that this was the best idea since sliced bread. Although Mum actually hates sliced bread, to be honest.

'You're far too young to go on holiday on your own,' snapped Mum. 'I'm glad about the job, that's fine, well done. But as for a holiday on your own – forget it!'

CHAPTER 6

My stomach tied itself in a knot, a gallon of red-hot adrenalin hurtled up my neck, and my hands curled themselves into iron fists.

'But you haven't even discussed it!' I yelled. 'You don't know anything about it!' Mum raised her hand, like a policeman stopping traffic.

'You're damn right I don't know anything about it,' she said in a quiet, steely voice. 'And that's the first of the many reasons why this is simply not on.'

'Well, let's discuss it now!' I demanded, grabbing the remote and switching off the TV. Mum looked quietly at me. We were sitting side by side on the sofa – a bit too close for a row, but I had to get on with it.

'Fine,' said Mum in calm-and-deadly mode (the worst). 'Where are you staying? Who's going with you? How much is it going to cost?'

She waited. I could feel myself blushing in panic as I realised I couldn't answer any of these questions properly.

'Everybody's going!' I flapped. 'Chloe, and Tobe and Ferg, and – and – and loads of people. Everybody goes to Newquay! Tam went to Newquay when she was my age!' I pointed dramatically and accusingly at Tam, who had backed towards the door and was about to escape.

'Tam was a year older,' said Mum swiftly. 'And she went with Kirsty and her family, as I recall.'

'Well, Chloe's mum might come!' I yelled recklessly. I knew this was a stupid thing to say, but I couldn't help myself. I was totally out of control. Tam was such an idiot to pitch me into this.

'Assuming she doesn't, though, where are you planning to stay?' enquired Mum. I hesitated. She arched a perfect eyebrow.

'We haven't decided yet!' I said. 'A surf lodge, probably.'

'And do they accept people your age travelling on their own?' asked Mum, as if she knew they didn't.

'We haven't done all the research yet!' I cried miserably.

'So how much money have you saved up for this?' she asked.

'I did have £137,' I said. 'But I gave some to the flood victims.' I was hoping Mum would admire me for my charity. 'But we're earning over £140 a week at the farm, so when we're finished I'll have £560, so I'll end up with about £640 altogether.'

For a split second Mum looked impressed that I was going to be so loaded. But instantly she reverted to negative mode.

'"A fool and her money are soon parted,"' she quipped icily. I hate those sneery proverbs.

'That's a bit rich coming from a woman who's just bought a pair of Jimmy Choo shoes!' I yelled. 'How much were they? £350?'

'£340,' said Mum sternly. 'And they were for Aunt Alice's funeral.'

'So it wasn't a treat for you, it was a tribute to Aunt Alice?' I sneered. 'Nice one.'

'Don't take that tone with me, please, Zoe,' snapped Mum. 'I've had a very trying day.'

'Well, I've had a very trying day too!' I shouted.

'Oh, for goodness' sake,' sighed Mum, lying back on the sofa and looking at the ceiling. She held up her hand again in the policeman gesture. This means

Be Quiet or Else. I didn't care. I had run out of things to say. I was now trying hard not to cry. 'I assume nothing's actually booked, yet?'

I didn't answer. I just stared sullenly at the carpet. 'I'll take that as an affirmative,' said Mum. 'If nothing's actually booked, then no harm's done. We'll see you get a nice holiday after you've finished your job at the farm. Chloe can come too.'

'What, you mean a family holiday?' I asked.

'Yes, why not?' said Mum brightly. 'It'll be lovely.'

I got up off the sofa and glared down at her.

'Forget it!' I said crisply, and walked out of the room. If she was going to tell me I could *forget* my holiday, she could freakin' well *forget* hers. I went up to my room and slammed the door.

My teddy bear, Bruce, was lying on his back on the bed with his legs in the air. I threw myself on my bed and cried into him for about five minutes. Eventually, though, I began to feel more angry than sad, and stopped crying. It took me five minutes with make-up remover wipes to deal with the mascara crisis. Then I started to plan. Bruce was giving me an encouraging smile. *Don't give up*, he seemed to be saying. *You'll think of something*.

I grabbed my mobile and rang Chloe on hers.

Voicemail. I rang her landline. Voicemail. I rang Toby. He replied right away.

'Tobe!' I cried. 'Disaster! My mum's said I can't go to Newquay!'

'Mine did at first,' said Toby. 'Don't worry, you can make her change her mind.'

'How did you manage it?'

'Well, I started with blackmail,' said Toby.

'*What!?*'

'I told her that if she didn't let me go, I'd tell Dad that she's only been to the gym three times. He shelled out big time for her membership.'

'But, Tobe! I don't know any of my mum's naughty secrets. And she's not nice and flexible like your mum.'

'You could stop eating,' suggested Toby. 'Parents get terrified when you do that.'

'Toby! When have you ever refused to eat?'

'I did once, when they said I couldn't go to Glastonbury.'

'How long did you refuse food for?'

'About half an hour.'

'Oh, come on, Tobe! Get serious! This is a major life crisis!'

'Just stop speaking to her,' he suggested. 'Go into a massive sulk.'

'I'm doing that already,' I said. 'But I can't keep it up for four weeks.'

'I think bribery works best,' said Toby. 'I promised my mum I'd wash the car every week, vacuum one room in the house every day, and clean out the fridge every Tuesday. Plus I'm mowing the lawn about twice a week and putting the bins out.'

'Tobe, you're an angel!' I cried. 'You deserve to go to New York for all that, never mind Newquay.'

I cheered up a bit, and went into planning mode again. We still had nowhere to stay. I asked Toby if he and Ferg had found anything yet.

'Not yet,' admitted Toby. 'But Ferg is on the case in every spare moment. We're planning to camp somewhere.'

The thought of camping by the sea was so wonderful that for a split second my eyes filled with tears of impossible longing. Then reality kicked in and I realised that camping would mean no bathroom, and even more crucial, no bathroom mirror. How could I deal with my mascara obligations and slosh enough cover-up on Nigel to keep him low profile without a bathroom mirror at my disposal 24/7?

What's more, my family went camping in Wales once, and it was so wet, my mum moved into a B&B

and wouldn't speak to my dad for a whole afternoon. Hmmm . . . camping wasn't really my style, I had to admit. If Toby and Fergus decided to camp somewhere, Chloe and I would just have to stay somewhere different. The four of us had discussed all the possible permutations a hundred times and it would be totally cool if they ended up camping and we were in a surf lodge.

But first, in order to get to Newquay at all, I had to soften Mum up somehow. I began to plan my campaign. It was no use losing it and yelling. I'd have to convince her that our hol in Newquay would be safe, fragrant, chaste and sober. Then I'd have to promise a huge amount of chores. If this didn't work I might have to resort to dark threats about the future. Unless she let me go to Newquay now, I would force her to wear beige and bright blue when she was old. I knew that would strike the most terrible fear into her soul.

CHAPTER 7

On Monday it was raining as Chloe and I trudged along the lane towards Old Hall Farm. I was wearing a cagoule I hadn't used for a year, and it was not only unattractively tight under the armpits, but smelt mysteriously of dragon's piss. I was going to have to rip it off and throw it over the nearest hedge, the minute I saw Oliver. Even if it was pouring with rain at the time.

I was thrilled at the thought of seeing Oliver today. But I didn't want to work myself up into a foam-flecked frenzy by talking about it all the time. Anyway, we urgently needed to work out a way of changing my mum's mind about Newquay. I had spent Sunday trying in vain to persuade her that our hol would involve mainly praying, going on long healthy walks and ingesting wholesome organic veg. It hadn't worked. Then I'd offered to clean the whole house from top to bottom, iron the carpets, scrub the books, de-flea the rugs and vacuum the toilets till they screamed for mercy, but she wasn't buying it.

'Tell her we're going with my mum,' said Chloe.

'I did actually mention that possibility,' I confessed. 'Even though I knew it was madness, cos she was bound to ring your mum and check up on us.'

'Maybe we could actually get my mum to go with us,' mused Chloe.

'But then we'd have your mum with us all the time!' I cried in dismay. 'I mean, I love your mum, she's great and stuff, but nobody goes to Newquay with their mum! I mean, we would be legendary retards from day one. People would point us out on the beach and snigger.'

'We could get her to rent a caravan with us,' said Chloe, going off on a foolish flight of fancy. 'And then when we get there we could drug her, you know – give her a potion, like in *Romeo and Juliet* – only one that lasts for a whole week, and she could wake up just in time to drive us home.'

'Yeah, imagine inviting two hunky surfers back to the caravan. *Do sit down, sorry about the random parent, don't worry, she's in a coma.*' I found it hard to enter into the joke, though. When my mum says no to something, it usually stays no, and I felt sick at the thought of our wicked hol in Newquay going down the pan.

Old Hall Farm loomed up ahead – a cluster of hideous barn-type buildings made from corrugated iron and concrete. Behind them we could see the roof of what looked like an old house with huge chimneys like gigantic chess pieces.

Suddenly two dogs appeared and raced up: one with a lot of mad prancing and ferocious barking, the other in a sinister sideways shimmying manner, with a satanic grin. I almost pooed my pants in fear. I'm a bit nervous of dogs at the best of times.

A huge man with a red beard appeared. 'Nan! Bunty!' he shouted. 'Come here!' The dogs turned round, though with longing backward looks at us, and joined him by the gate.

'I love your dogs!' said Chloe. 'They're so cute!' She walked right up to them and started to stroke them. OK, she has her own dog, so she's a bit more dog-savvy. I decided to stay back a bit, and pretended I was having trouble with the zip of my cagoule. 'We're Chloe and Zoe,' she said. I felt awkward: after all, I'd been the one who'd rung Martin and fixed it all up. But as Chloe had been so iffy about working on the farm, it was kind of good news that she was already bonding with the guy in the Barbour.

'Zoe's a bit scared of dogs,' explained Chloe, looking back at me and grinning.

I felt like a total idiot, cowering by the gate. I made a mental note to sign up for a dog-handling class at night school.

'It's OK!' boomed Martin. 'They don't bite! It's me you want to worry about!' We laughed nervously, and I stepped forward a tad.

Two thin men appeared. 'Martin!' shouted one in a foreign accent. 'Tractor is tyre flat! Is puncture, where is spanner?'

'In the tractor cab!' yelled Martin, looking harassed.

'Spanner not in cab!' said the smaller guy. He was looking at us with a friendly smile. I smiled back, even though I didn't want to indicate that marriage was a possibility. His head was too round for my taste, his nose too short, his ears too large, and his eyebrows met in the middle in a way I associate with mass murder.

'Zoe and Chloe,' said Martin briskly, 'this is

Zxltyvsek and Proszchak. From Poland.' I don't know how you would spell their names in English, but that's what it sounded like, anyway.

'Hello, good evening!' said the shorter one (Prozac, at a guess). His greeting was bizarre as it was barely nine o'clock in the morning. They shook hands with us.

'Hi, how's it going?' asked Chloe. 'You speak great English!' Chloe seemed to be taking all the initiatives. I was grateful, to tell you the truth. I was not made for country life. I was born in high heels and Mum's breast milk was ninety-per-cent decaf latte. I had only come here in order to see Oliver. So where the hell was he?

Silkvest and Prozac seemed very friendly, and Chloe was soaking up the Polish admiration. I hoped she wouldn't get a thing about one of them, because the other would be bound to think I was his.

'Right.' Martin solved the spanner problem and then turned back to us. 'Hop in the Land Rover. I'll take you to the field. I'm afraid you're going to get wet this morning, girls. God, this weather! If this goes on much longer, the spuds'll be ruined.'

All three of us were jammed into the front of the Land Rover. It had the filthiest windscreen I had ever seen, smeared with the dung of three different species, I swear. The torments I endured for Oliver!

'OK,' said Martin, 'Brendan will tell you what to do.' A figure appeared in the distance, through the mist and rain. 'He's on his gap year,' said Martin. 'Watch out, he's a bit of a ladykiller. Brendan!' he yelled. 'Here's Chloe and Zoe – pricking out lettuces, OK?'

We climbed out, Martin drove off and Brendan walked up. Though I was annoyed with him for not being Oliver, I could clearly see that he was a rustic dreamboat. He was wearing moss-green togs and his eyes were moss-green, too. His face was tanned. His hair was brown and curly.

'Hi there,' he said, in a faintly Irish accent. I so love Irish voices. 'Terrible day, isn't it? Don't worry, though, I've ordered some sunshine for later.'

He led us through the rain to a vast expanse of lettuces in a swamp. 'Pricking out,' said Brendan. I didn't like the sound of it. I knew I was going to hurt myself.

'Here's the little darlings,' said Brendan playfully, indicating a row of baby lettuces about as high as a little finger. 'There's about four hundred in this row, but they've got to be dug up, separated . . .'

Bending down, he illustrated the process. Basically we were transplanting the lettuces on to another bed, so each little baby had a nice big area of soil all to itself. This was what we had to do all morning, in the rain. And there was no sign of Oliver. I would rather have been doing even *maths*.

'Great weather for it.' Brendan grinned. Raindrops were caught on his eyelashes. 'We won't have to water them, though, with any luck. I'll be back to collect you at one o'clock – spot of lunch in the farm-house, OK?'

'Will Oliver be there?' I asked, trying to sound casual but ending up strangled and weird. 'We know him from school. That's how we got this job.'

'Ah, Oliver's usually with Martin,' said Brendan. 'He does a fair bit of tractor work, too. He should be there at lunchtime, though.'

For the next hour we knelt in puddles, dabbling in the mud and fiddling with baby lettuces, while the rain ran down our necks. Several times I touched a worm or a slug, and shrieked aloud. But I endured it all because I knew that in only a couple of hours, I would be seeing Oliver.

'This is a freakin' nightmare,' groaned Chloe, sitting back on her heels after the two hundred and fiftieth lettuce. 'I'd rather eat rocks than work here a moment longer.'

'Hang in there, babe!' I had to head off this mutiny, though secretly I sympathised with Chloe. In fact, I was worse off than she was – she'd got water-proofs on, head-to-toe, and a waterproof hat. I was literally soaked to the skin. 'Only two more hours till lunch! And Brendan said it was going to clear up this afternoon!'

'Zoe,' said Chloe with a kind of deadly rage, 'if we were working for Major Events we'd be indoors – dressed in cute black skirts and handing out canapés to millionaires.'

'Stick with it, please!' I begged. 'I'll make it up to you, I promise!'

'And they're paying what exactly for this torment?'

'I can't remember exactly!' I tried to look wacky and disorganised, but it didn't work. My face twitched guiltily.

'Yes you can!' Chloe yelled. She had smelt a rat. 'How much!?'

'£3.50 an hour,' I admitted. 'I know it's low but it's the standard wage for people our age, apparently.'

'Low?' shrieked Chloe. 'It's slave labour! £3.50! I can't believe this! You are so sneaky it's just not true!'

'Chloe, I only –'

'Shut up!' yelled Chloe. 'You never told me it was £3.50! That's peanuts! How could you do this?'

'Oliver –'

'I'm sick of freakin' Oliver! We're getting drowned here! This job is pants! We could be working indoors doing lovely parties with Major Events for £4.20! I don't believe it! Well, you can wallow in mud and rain for a month if you like, but I've had enough. I'm handing in my notice at the end of the day – Oliver or no Oliver.'

Chloe flounced off down the row of lettuces and ignored me for the next two hours. I let her go. I was hoping she'd cool down by lunchtime. I had to admit that the work was torture, but I had to put up with it if it meant I'd be seeing Oliver every day. But what if Chloe really did give in her notice: would I be able to hack it here on my own? The thought was too awful for words.

CHAPTER 8

By lunchtime we must have pricked out millions of lettuces, and we were steaming gently as the sun took over from the rain. Then the Land Rover appeared. This time Brendan was driving it.

'Hop in!' he said. 'God! What a morning! I thought I was a rain-lover, but I'm beginning to change my mind.' We piled into the front beside him. There wasn't much room; in fact Chloe had to sit kind of half on my knee, which is awkward if you aren't really on speaking terms.

'What have you been doing?' I enquired, trying to sound chic and playful, like somebody at a cocktail party.

'Treating maggoty sheep,' said Brendan. 'I've got a way with them.' Chloe and I screamed in unison.

Brendan laughed. 'Sorry about that,' he said, glancing sideways at us with a roguish grin. 'I know it doesn't do much for a fella's charm. Mind you, some of the things I've had to do on this farm you wouldn't wish on your worst enemy.'

It was only a short drive back to the farmhouse. My heart started to lurch giddily at the thought of seeing Oliver. However, I have rarely looked more unattractive: my hair was soaking wet and plastered to my skull and my jeans were literally dripping.

The house was amazing, though: huge and old and rambling, built out of mellow brick, with those towering chimneys. It looked like something out of a period drama – a perfect setting for Oliver, possibly in a long black riding coat and highwayman's boots.

'Come round the back,' said Brendan. 'Nobody ever uses the front door, anyway.'

We arrived at a big porch, where we took off our wellies, and then Brendan led us into a vast kitchen, with high beams from which bunches of herbs and black old saucepans were hanging. There was no sign of Oliver. A middle-aged woman was sitting at the table reading *Private Eye*.

'Oh my God!!' she exclaimed. 'I lost all track of time!' She whipped off her glasses and lost control of them. They flew across the kitchen and landed in a dog bowl, in which the remains of a dog's dinner was still horribly visible. 'Cripes!' said the woman, like somebody in an old-fashioned comic. She picked up her glasses and took them to the tap to be rinsed. 'I'm so sorry!' She turned and looked us up and down. 'You poor things, you're so wet!'

'This is Zoe and Chloe,' said Brendan. 'They've done sterling work in the field all morning.' She dried her glasses, put them back on, and came round the table to us, smiling. Unfortunately she had missed a bit of dog-meat jelly, which was clinging to the side of the glasses and wobbled distractingly when she moved.

'I'm Sarah, Martin's wife,' she said. 'Well, slave, actually. Are you really terribly wet?' She looked at my jeans. 'You haven't got waterproofs? Oh dear! Did nobody warn you?'

'We only fixed it up last night,' I said. 'I spoke to Martin.'

'You must have some dry trousers!' said Sarah. 'You'll catch your death of cold! Come on!' And she marched me out of the kitchen and up the stairs just as, behind us, the back door was opening. I could hear Martin booming away and Chloe's voice saying,

'Oh, hi, Oliver!' He'd arrived! But I'd missed him!

'Come into our bedroom a minute,' said Sarah. It was the size of Oxfordshire. 'You see that door? That's our en suite. Have a shower – use any towels. I'll find something for you to wear, but I'm afraid it might be a size fourteen.'

'That's fine!' I assured her. 'I am a size fourteen!' I wished it was a lie.

The bathroom was antique but divine. Although desperate to see Oliver, I did realise that I would look less repulsive after a shower. It had a big old brass shower head that looked as if it had once been on a Victorian watering can. I showered for England, and I was drying myself when suddenly a door flew open in the panelling – an extra door I hadn't previously noticed – and a girl stood there. She was petite and wearing a green dress. In the film of our lives she would be played by Scarlett Johansson.

'Oh my God!' she said. 'I'm so sorry. I thought you were Mum.' She turned abruptly and went out again. I hastily put on my T-shirt and undies, then I wrapped a towel around my waist and crept out into Sarah's bedroom again.

She had left a pair of chinos in a kind of dung colour folded up on the bed, together with a handy hairdryer already plugged in. I put the chinos on (five out of ten for style – they made my bum look like a strange mushroom), then I blasted hot air at my head for three minutes, and went downstairs.

There was merry laughter from the kitchen and I was desperate to join in, though concerned that I was damp and mushroomy when I should have been irresistible and chic.

Martin was sitting at the head of the table, and Oliver was on his right, with his back to me. Everybody was drinking soup and eating baguettes. It was kind of crowded, with the Polish guys in there as well, and there was only one place to sit: down at the far end of the table away from Oliver, and on the same side of the table, which meant that in order just to catch a fleeting glimpse of his fingertips I'd have to dislocate my neck.

Sarah asked if I would like some soup. I could hardly refuse, even though it was an unsettling green colour and contained strange lumps.

Actually it did taste rather nice. It was also hot, which helped.

'I make it once a year, in the autumn,' said Sarah, 'and I just go on boiling it up and adding seasonal veg to it, day after day.'

'It's delicious!' I exclaimed politely, while fighting off sudden nausea. This soup was at least eight months old!

I bolted down the last of the soup and then got stuck into a ham baguette. Safer ground. I was just beginning to feel a bit more comfortable. Brendan and Sarah were discussing Great Rainstorms of the Past. I swear, if I live to be a hundred, I will never take part in such a boring conversation.

'OK, Oliver,' said Martin, finishing off his tea. 'Off you go and move that electric fencing – then after that we're going to take those sheep off to Grange Ground.' There was the sound of Oliver getting up. This was a disaster! He was leaving already and we hadn't exchanged a single word – or even a look.

Oliver drifted picturesquely over to the dishwasher and loaded his plates (so divinely domestic and helpful!) and then paused by the door for a moment.

'Cheers, then,' he said, and ran his eyes over the assembled company. Was it my imagination, or did his eyes kind of linger on me for a split second? 'Thanks for the lunch, Sarah!' he said – and was gone.

'Such lovely manners!' said Sarah approvingly, smiling fondly at her baguette.

'Yeah, Oliver's a legend!' Chloe grinned. 'Half the school is mad about him – especially Zoe!'

My heart gave a sickening jolt. I looked up. Everybody was grinning at me. Even the Polish guys seemed to have understood. I felt my face go deepest crimson. I was never going to speak to Chloe again.

CHAPTER 9

'I'd be mad about him if I was your age!' said Sarah, moving swiftly to rescue me from my embarrassment.

'I'd be mad about him if I was a girl!' added Brendan.

'Well, I'm not mad about him,' I retorted, glaring at Chloe. 'I admit I did have a crush on him once, but that was in Year Nine.' I'd blushed deeply so it was kind of useless to lie. 'I think my sister had the hots for him, though – big time.'

'Oh, you've got a sister?' exclaimed Sarah, tactfully grabbing the new subject. 'What does she do?'

'She's at uni,' I said.

'Oh, where?' asked Sarah. We then discussed Tam for a few minutes, and she told us all about her daughter Lily's brilliant career at Oxford. I assumed

Lily was the girl who'd barged into the bathroom. I boasted right back about Tam's intelligence, though secretly remembering her evil plan to pretend to be ill so she wouldn't have to go to Granny's. Sometimes I think she doesn't deserve my unflagging PR efforts on her behalf.

Chloe then started raving about my parents, going on about how chic my mum was and how clever and amusing my dad was and stuff. Chloe really loves my family. I feel sorry for her, because she's an only child and I sometimes think she's embarrassed about her mostly absent dad and the way her mum surfs the astrological websites and plays with her tarot pack.

When we went out again after lunch, the rain had stopped and the sun was revving up nicely. I was glad, because it might have made Chloe like the farm more, but on the other hand, I was still furious with her for telling everybody I was mad about Oliver. So after Brendan had taken us to a polytunnel and showed us how to prick out more baby plants, we worked in total silence. I wondered who was going to apologise first. I had a nasty feeling it would have to be me, because I so desperately wanted Chloe not to hand in her notice.

After a while Brendan dropped by to see how we were getting on and we started chatting.

'Where are you going to uni?' asked Chloe.

'Edinburgh,' said Brendan. 'I did think of going to Dublin but it would be too near home. You don't want your family breathing down your neck when you're out and about making a nuisance of yourself, now, do you? Not that I plan to misbehave. I'm famous for my religious devotion and tidy habits.' He twinkled at both of us.

'What subject are you doing?' asked Chloe.

'Time-wasting and binge drinking,' Brendan grinned. Chloe laughed hysterically. I just smiled. OK, it was funny, but it wasn't that funny. 'Veterinary science, officially,' he added. 'Same as Oliver. Although I think he may be having second thoughts.'

'Second thoughts?' I asked. 'Why?'

'I'm not sure he's a hundred per cent motivated,' said Brendan with a shrug. 'Just a little feeling I get sometimes.' Shortly after, he went off, leaving us to be baked alive in the polytunnel.

After Brendan had gone, I decided it was time for a showdown. I didn't want to put Chloe off working here, obviously, but she had to play ball.

'Chloe,' I said as tactfully as I could, 'I was really

embarrassed when you told everybody at lunch that I was mad about Oliver.'

Chloe whirled round unexpectedly. 'Listen!' she snapped. 'I've had it up to here with this crap job. I was soaked through this morning, now I'm getting boiled alive. You can keep coming, as you seem to like it so much, but you can count me out.'

'Chloe!' I wailed. 'Don't be stupid! We've got to keep coming! I told Martin we could work for a month! And, anyway, it's amazing! All the animals and stuff! And really funny people! You've got to stick it out! Don't give up on me!'

At this point Silkvest and Prozac entered the polytunnel, and started to mess about with the tomato plants. It was impossible for Chloe and me to continue our row. This was a shame. Every row should end with somebody flouncing off and slamming doors, followed, after a decent interval, by a weepy reunion and hot buttered toast.

After boiling in the polytunnel all afternoon, with Chloe and me sulking away at each other in stereo, I had a vile headache. But of course, I had to keep up a charade that everything was hunky-dory. OK, I had only glimpsed Oliver so far, but I was sure there would be lots of tender moments among the haystacks. If there were any haystacks.

At the end of the afternoon Chloe went off in the direction of the outdoor loo. The Polish guys had gone. I heard footsteps cross the yard. Was it Oliver? My heart missed a beat. If it was Oliver, he was going to see me in Sarah's horrendous, lumpy, dung-coloured chinos.

But it was Brendan who entered the polytunnel. He looked closely at me.

'What's wrong, Zoe?' he asked. His voice had lost that hard kidding-around edge and sounded soft and concerned. 'I'm famous for my ability to read people's body language.'

'I've got a horrible headache,' I said. 'It's really hot in here.'

Brendan looked sympathetic. 'Poor Zoe,' he said. 'You've worked so hard, too.' Suddenly he placed his hand across my brow. It was deliciously cool. He kept it there for several seconds. It was soothing to my head, but he was basically the wrong guy.

'Nice cool hands,' I said. He nodded.

'Always at your disposal,' he said quietly. 'My hands are cool in summer and warm in winter – I've had no complaints.' There was something about this remark I didn't much like, but there was no time to think about it now, because Oliver had suddenly arrived.

Brendan removed his hand – not guiltily, just tactfully. But Oliver must have seen him stroking my head.

'Poor Zoe's got an awful headache,' said Brendan. 'It's too hot to be working in here all afternoon.'

'Oh,' said Oliver, frowning. 'As a matter of fact, I've got a headache too.'

'Let's get you some painkillers from the kitchen,' said Brendan. It was five thirty anyway – the time we were due to finish. Sarah was sitting at the kitchen table reading a book and jumped when we entered. She certainly seemed to be a jumpy woman.

'Oh, cripes!' she gasped. 'Zoe, I totally forgot about washing your jeans! I was going to wash and dry them for you but I got distracted by this book about unusual vegetables! I'm so sorry!'

'Don't worry! I've got loads of pairs at home.'

'Zoe and Oliver have both got headaches,' said Brendan. 'OK if I give them some paracetamol?'

'Oh yes, of course,' exclaimed Sarah. 'I'm so sorry. That damned polytunnel is an inferno. Why Martin didn't put you in there this morning, and out in the field this afternoon, I don't know. He's hopeless!'

Brendan handed out the pills and Oliver and I swallowed them. We had shared our first paracetamol! I only hoped that, in due course, it would lead to a night at the theatre followed by dinner at a posh restaurant. After that Oliver got out his car keys. Apparently he wasn't dependent on bus timetables like us.

'I'd give you a lift,' he said uncomfortably, 'but I live in the other direction.' There was silence for a split second. I almost wished he hadn't said anything at all. It would have been better if he'd driven off without a backward look. But maybe he was just shy, and he thought we'd think he was trying to pull or something.

'I'll give you a lift to the bus stop,' Brendan cut in quickly. 'It's too hot to walk, especially with a headache. And I have to go to the village shop, anyway, for some toothpaste.'

As Brendan drove, he did some impressions of Martin's booming voice. 'Imagine how he'd be as a beautician!' he grinned. *'Do you want yer bloomin' eyebrows plucked or not? And don't fidget for God's sake or I'll have to tie yer down! Pass me that rope, Brendan!'*

On the bus on the way home, Chloe turned to me with a mysterious expression on her face.

'Zoe,' she said, 'I'm sorry about the row. I decided not to chuck in the job yet. I'll give it till the end of the week. And I'm sorry I told them you fancied Oliver. I was still feeling really annoyed about the wages and everything.'

'Sorry I didn't tell you about the muns,' I said. 'I was terrified you wouldn't want to work on the farm if you knew, and I was so desperate to be with Oliver . . .'

We had a quick hug and then Chloe suddenly produced a naughty grin. 'Tell me,' she said, 'Brendan . . . how many out of ten for sex appeal?' I suddenly saw a brilliant opportunity.

'If Oliver didn't exist,' I said, 'nine and a half! And I reckon he's got the hots for you!'

Chloe frowned, but it was a kind of smiley frown with a secret agenda. 'No,' she said. 'Do you really think so?'

'Defo!' I assured her. 'You should see the way he looks at you – when you're not looking.'

'Oh, well,' said Chloe with a mischievous smirk, 'maybe life at the farm isn't going to be a hundred per cent torment after all.'

CHAPTER 10

When I got home, Tam was lying on the sofa, watching a documentary about Hitler.

'Zoe!' she called as I passed the door of the sitting room. 'Come here! How was your day?' I slouched in and perched on the arm of the sofa. My head was still pounding. The TV was deafening. Hitler was ranting away like mad.

'Turn it down!' I grumbled. 'I've got a vile headache from working in the goddam polytunnel all afternoon.'

'Not good, then?' asked Tam, trying to pull me down on to the sofa.

'No.' I resisted being pulled. 'I'm going to get a smoothie and have a lie down.'

'Listen! Zoe! Wait! Mum will be back in a minute.

I'm going to tell her I've got this terrible pain. I have got a pain, anyway, actually, so it's not a complete lie.'

'What?!'

'No, I've got to. I can't go and see Granny now. It's impossible. I can see her later. Listen. I've got to see Ed again. It's difficult. We have to keep it secret. Zoe, don't tell anybody, but . . . this is really awkward, but . . . he's married!' Her voice dropped to a melodramatic whisper. My heart froze.

'Married?!' I exploded. 'Are you *insane*?'

'Shush!' Tam hissed in panic, grabbing my hand. I pulled away from her and backed towards the door, shaking my head in disbelief.

'I'm going upstairs,' I said quietly. 'I've got a headache. A *real* one.'

'Zoe! Look – take an aspirin or something, we can't both be ill at the same time.'

'Unlike you,' I snapped, 'I really am in pain. I can't believe you! You want me to heroically hide my headache so you can take centre stage with your so-called stomach ache. Well, tough. I'm going. The TV is hurting my eyes.'

'Zoe! Wait!' Tam flicked off the TV. 'I really have got a pain! It's not fictional!' I ignored her, collected an ice-cold smoothie from the fridge, and stomped upstairs. It was just typical of Tam to play the drama queen. The minute Mum got in, Tam would be sprawling all over the sofa and groaning in agony. Well, I wasn't having any part of it.

I would have slammed my bedroom door if my head hadn't hurt so much. I ripped off Sarah's ghastly chinos and lay down on my bed with Bruce the Bear, stared at the ceiling, and tried to get to grips with the awful news that Tam's boyfriend was married. How could she be so stupid? What if he had kids and everything? How could it possibly turn out well? It just couldn't. Somebody – possibly everybody – was going to get hurt.

I went into one of my nightmare scenarios. I imagined that the phone would ring. I would pick it up. A woman with a very snappy voice would say, '*Who's this?*' I would identify myself, feeling angsty. '*I'm looking for somebody called Tamsin,*' she would snarl. '*She's out – can I take a message?*' I would stammer nervously. '*Well, tell her to keep away from my husband or I'll come round and hit her with his cricket bat!*' Later (in my fantasy) a cricket ball came whizzing through the window and struck Dad on the temple just as he was dishing up a divine onion gratin. Dad was brain damaged, which was a shame, because up till then he'd been the only member of our family who was really interested in cooking.

I felt sick with dread. I turned over on my side and tried to think about something else. I hadn't had a meaningful conversation with Oliver today. But it was handy that Brendan was working there, because Chloe seemed quite taken with him. It could work out nicely, just as long as I managed to limit my exposure to the dogs (frightening) and the slugs (disgusting). My worst nightmare would be a dog-sized slug called Bonzo who would jump up and lick my face when I got home.

After ten minutes I got up, pulled on my comfy old jeans and fetched a damp facecloth to drape over my brow. It did help a little, and I dropped into a slight doze. I suppose I was a bit tired from all that farm work. Suddenly I was in a divine wood with Oliver. He took my hand and said, 'I'm going to show you my secret den where I live when I'm not working for the government.' We pushed through loads of bushes and after a while we came to the dearest little cottage, in a slight clearing but surrounded by trees. It had turf on the roof. It looked like an illustration from a children's book.

'It's the sort of place where a witch might live,' I

said. Oliver seemed to have turned into someone else. He was slightly on the cusp of himself and Mr Scott, who teaches sport at school.

'Zoe, can you keep a secret?' he asked, holding me close and looking down into my eyes.

'Yes!' I panted. This was ace. I didn't much care whether he was Oliver or Mr Scott, to be honest, I was just up for it, no matter what.

'The fact is,' Oliver whispered, 'I *am* a witch!' And suddenly we both kind of flew up into the air, the sky exploded, and I heard Mum's voice outside my bedroom door.

'I'm going to ring an ambulance!' she was shouting. 'I don't like the look of her at all! It could be appendicitis!'

'I think you're over-reacting, but if that's what you want to do, go ahead,' came Dad's voice. I sat up quickly. The pain in my head returned with a sickening lurch.

'I am *not* over-reacting!' shouted Mum. 'I'm going to ring them now! Come down and sit with her!' There was the sound of footsteps going downstairs, and raised voices below. I got up. OK, this was all a big charade, but I couldn't help wanting to see it for myself.

Tam was lying on the sofa stretched out stiffly, clutching her abdomen. Dad was hanging about nearby, trying to look supportive. Mum was talking on the phone in the kitchen – to the emergency services.

'What's wrong?' I asked. 'Period pain?'

'No!' snapped Tam, giving me a fierce flashing glare. 'It's worse than that! Mum's calling an ambulance!'

'I don't think it's anything dangerous,' said Dad. 'But Mum just wanted to be on the safe side . . .'

Mum came in now, totally ignored me and threw herself down on her knees before the sacred sofa where Saint Tamsin was writhing in agony.

'Hang on, darling, they'll be here in ten minutes,' said Mum, grabbing Tam's hand and massaging it. Hang on? What was this, a deathbed? Sudden unexpected childbirth, possibly the Second Coming?

It was plainly not the moment to tackle Mum again on the subject of my hol in Newquay. I would have to save up my threats, pleadings, promises and tantrums for later. I went out to the kitchen and poured myself another smoothie. I know they're full of calories but I just couldn't help it. Moments later Mum came bustling in.

'Oh, Zoe!' she said, as if she'd totally forgotten I existed. 'Run up and get a set of clean pyjamas for poor Tam, quick! In the airing cupboard. Or a nightie. And her dressing gown.'

'I've got a headache,' I said plaintively. Mum frowned and flared the whites of her eyes at me. She only does this when really wild with rage.

'Why must you always try and compete all the time?' she snapped. 'Don't be so silly! Tam could be seriously ill! Do as I ask, please! Now!'

CHAPTER 11

I went upstairs and found the least flattering pyjamas I could – quite a hard task as Tam is such a style queen and she could look good in a tarpaulin. I was furious, though. How dare Mum question my one-hundred-per-cent real headache (caused by back-breaking toil) while she crooned over Tam's false pains (caused by an illicit amour)? Although of course I was desperate for my headache to clear, in another way I wanted it to get worse and worse until my head burst, releasing spaghetti hoops and bits of brain all over Mum's freshly laundered linen.

Soon the ambulance arrived and, amazingly enough, Tam was taken away in it, accompanied by Mum, who was clutching at her hand in feverish terror. Dad and I stayed at home.

'Well,' said Dad. 'What a hoo-hah. Don't worry, I don't think it's anything serious. Are you OK, Zoe?' he asked, putting his arm round my shoulders. 'You look a bit pale, old boy.' Dad sometimes calls me that. It's a kind of joke about how he and Mum thought I was a boy – until I was born, obviously.

'I've got a horrible headache,' I said. Dad stroked my brow a bit and gradually my rage started to ebb away. Then I told him all about my day at the farm, and Dad sat me down and made me egg and chips (my favourite, which we're never allowed to eat when Mum is home).

After supper, because it was one of those long, light evenings, Dad and I sat out on the patio and sipped some lemonade and I asked him all about holidays he'd had when he was a teenager. This was to soften him up and get him on my side when, once this Tam melo-drama was over, I would mention Newquay again.

Dad told me that when he was fourteen, he and his friend Tony had gone on their bikes, camping in the Forest of Dean. Just the two of them! And they'd only been *fourteen*! Right. That was terrific news. I filed it away to use against him later. Though I do love Dad dearly, it's always as well to prepare for a long campaign.

Mum rang to say the docs thought Tam didn't have appendicitis, but they were keeping her in overnight just to be on the safe side. It was just as Dad had predicted. I was impressed, as usual, by my dad's calmness and insight, compared to Mum's deluded hysterics.

'She says they think Tam's probably got an irritable bowel,' said Dad. Well, almost right. As far as I was concerned, Tam *was* an irritable bowel. Just think, while that ambulance was taking her to hospital, somebody really ill might have died. I was so tempted to tell Dad that the only thing Tam was suffering from was adultery.

After sitting around on the patio for a while, I began to feel restless. I told Dad I was going for a stroll to clear my head. I felt heaps better since the egg and chips, obviously, but there was still a little niggle and I was sure a walk in the park would cure it.

I love the park. There's so much space and it's for everybody, but at this time of day - late evening in summer, with the sun low and romantic in the trees – it was mainly joggers, and teenagers chilling out. I began to feel heaps better, even though I was still disgusted with Tam and her stupid charade – and her crazy fixation on Married Ed. Hopeless!

'Hey, Zoe!' I looked round. Somebody was waving to me from under a tree. It was Jess Jordan. Great! I could do with a laugh. I went over. Her boyfriend, Fred Parsons, was there too. They were surrounded by pieces of paper covered with scribbled notes.

'What's all this?' I asked.

'Oh, just trying to write comedy sketches,' said Jess. 'Are you OK, Zoe? You look a bit stressed out.'

'It's nothing, really,' I told her. 'I've got a bit of a headache, plus I'm pissed off with my sister. She's pretending to have appendicitis because she's involved with a married man – don't tell anybody, for God's sake.'

'Of course we won't tell,' said Jess. 'Fred, hand me my mobile! What's Jackie Blabbermouth's number again?'

'Why resort to appendicitis, though?' asked Fred. 'Is he a surgeon or something? *Darling* . . .' Fred put on a posh surgeon's voice. '*We've got to stop meeting like this – I've taken out most of your organs already.*'

I giggled edgily. Although I'd wanted to have a laugh, I hadn't intended us to be laughing at this particular subject.

'It's not really funny,' I sighed, sitting down. 'I

mean, it's so, like, totally stupid of her to get involved with him. And now she's trying to get out of going to Granny's by pretending to have appendicitis! Just so she can skulk around with him!'

'Chill, Zoe!' said Jess. 'So your sister's stupid? At least you've *got* a sister. And it's better that she shouldn't really have appendicitis. Ben Jones had it, remember? He was absent for weeks.'

'Still harping on about Ben Jones!' snapped Fred, pretending to be jealous. At least, I think he was pretending. Jess turned to him with a shake of the head and a kind of fatigued smile.

'I'm not harping on about him,' she said. 'So stop being so jealous! I'm merely mentioning his appendicitis.'

'She's never really got over him,' Fred whispered confidingly. 'She bid for his appendix on eBay.'

'I would have won it too,' said Jess, 'but Flora beat me to it. She's had it mounted in silver and made into a hair slide.'

'So.' I was feeling a lot better already. Jess and Fred are guaranteed to lift your mood. They're going to be the next big thing in comedy. 'What are all these pieces of paper?'

'We're writing a sketch,' Jess explained. 'Only it's

rubbish.' She peered at me closely. 'Are you OK, Zoe? Really?'

'Oh, it's just a bit of a headache,' I said. 'Chloe and I are working on a farm and we had our first day today, and we were in this boiling polytunnel all afternoon.'

'We're working for Major Events,' said Jess. 'You know – the hospitality business.'

'Oh yes!' My heart lurched guiltily at the mention of Chloe's preferred work option. 'The company Beast Hawkins is working for, right? What do they do? Organise parties and stuff?'

'You bet!' Jess grinned. 'So our summer is just one mad round of pleasure! You should see Fred in his tux! He looks almost human.'

'Cruel but true,' said Fred. 'If you're thinking of getting married, we'd be happy to hand out the canapés.'

'Somehow,' I said with a hollow laugh, 'I don't think I'll be getting married, like, ever.'

'Nor will I!' Jess declared. 'I'm going to get divorced a few times, though – think of all the alimony!'

The mention of divorce made me a tad uneasy. On the way home I had a dreadful nightmare scenario involving Tam being murdered by her married man's crazed wife, who was played in the fantasy by Christina Ricci at her most sinister.

When I got home I found that Mum had returned, pale and tragic but relieved. She and Dad were sitting in the kitchen, drinking tea. As I entered she looked up with a sudden start, as if she'd forgotten I existed *again*.

'Zoe!' she said. 'The good news is, Tam hasn't got appendicitis.'

'I know that already,' I sighed. For one thing, Mum had rung us earlier to tell us. And for another, I'd known all along that what Tam was suffering from was something that mere surgery could not cure.

'How's your headache, sweetheart?' asked Dad, looking up from his sports page.

'Better, thanks, Dad,' I purred, walking round behind him and cuddling his shoulders.

'She's probably coming home tomorrow,' said Mum, still not picking up on my tragic headache. She was filing her nails with anxious energy.

'Well, I'm going to have an early night,' I said. 'Got to get up early for work tomorrow.'

'Oh yes!' said Mum. 'Sorry, darling, I'd forgotten it was your first day at the farm. How did it go?'

'Fine.' I shrugged. I didn't want to tell Mum any more. She wasn't my favourite parent at the moment. I sometimes think she's completely fixated on Tam. I was so tempted to say, 'Actually, you might be interested to know that Tam's staged this illness to get out of that lovely trip to Granny's which you set up for her – because she'd rather be skulking round secretly making whoopee with her new lover, the married man.'

But I'm not a *complete* bitch.

CHAPTER 12

The next morning Chloe was waiting at the bus stop. She looked at me from under her clouds of red hair, like a shy peeping woodland creature hiding in a hedge. Usually she plaits her hair back, so it's out of her face. She looked wonderful. I wondered if she'd made more of an effort so she could dazzle Brendan. I had applied three coats of mascara, myself, in case I got a chance to exchange a smouldering gaze with Oliver.

'How's your headache, Zoe?' she asked.

'Gone, thanks!' I beamed. 'I'm a hundred per cent OK and ready to rock!'

We had a laugh on the bus awarding imaginary prizes to everyone at the farm. Martin won it for Best Organic Beard in Show. Sarah won it for Dog Food as Personal Adornment.

'What about Brendan?' I asked, with a teasing wink.

'Official Sex God for Rural Areas!' Chloe grinned.

Despite our eager anticipation, there was no sign of Brendan or Oliver at the farm, and Martin sent us off to a field to do some weeding.

'I've brought a picnic today,' announced Chloe as we arrived in the field and surveyed the rows and rows of weed-infested veg. 'I couldn't face the thought of that soup again. I made some tuna and cucumber for you.'

'Oh, thanks, darlin', that's ace! I'll bring something tomorrow.'

We'd both come equipped for any eventuality, weather-wise. Mum had lent me her third-best panama hat. (She was saving the best two for herself and Tam, obviously.) I unrolled it and placed it on my head. I was already wearing wraparound sunglasses.

'What do you think of my hat?' I asked.

'You look like an aristocratic lesbian in *Miss Marple*!' giggled Chloe. 'Here's mine!' She pulled a weird khaki canvas-style hat out of her bag. She also lathered herself in SPF 1,000,000 sun cream, sprayed a bit of anti-bug stuff over both of us, and put on her own sunglasses.

'How do I look, then?' she demanded.

'Private eye on safari!' I said. 'Quite stylish in a retro kind of way. In the film, you'll be played by Gillian Anderson. Only she'll have to have a perm.'

'And you'll be played by Rachel Weisz,' said Chloe. 'But who'll play Brendan?'

'Jesse Metcalf,' I suggested. 'He's hot in an outdoorsy sort of way.'

'Yeah!' agreed Chloe. 'He could weed my cabbage patch any day. Who'll play Oliver?'

'Hmm . . . none of the Hollywood hunks are worthy,' I mused. 'Oliver will have to play himself.'

We identified a row of carrots, sat down beside it and started real weeding, trying to look as much as possible like Gillian Anderson and Rachel Weisz.

'How's Tam?' asked Chloe suddenly. I still hadn't told Chloe about Tam's absurd 'appendicitis' scare last night, because I was kind of ashamed of Tam at the moment. But I had to come clean now.

'Guess what,' I told Chloe. 'This is kind of tacky, but Tam's involved with a married man.'

'*What?!*' gasped Chloe.

'Plus,' I went on, 'she's so totally besotted with him that she staged an attack of fictional appendicitis last night rather than go to stay with Granny.'

'You're kidding!' breathed Chloe. 'My God! Tam is so daring! This guy must be a five-star hunk!'

'He must be a loser,' I retorted. I didn't want Chloe to treat this Tam business as a rather stylish joke. Chloe adores Tam, which is fine, as long as she adores me even more and is basically on my side whenever there's a fight between me and Tam. 'And if he's seeing Tam behind his wife's back, it won't be long before he's seeing somebody else behind Tam's back.'

'You don't *know* that,' argued Chloe. 'It might just be that she's going to be the love of his life. My dad was married to Caroline when he met my mum.' Whoops! I'd forgotten about Caroline. Mind you, Chloe's dad has started to spend all his time out in the Middle East, so I don't think Chloe's mum can still be quite the love of his life as much as she was in the early days.

'Hmmm. Maybe you're right,' I admitted. 'I suppose you can't be in love with two people at the same time – can you?'

'Sometimes,' twinkled Chloe naughtily, 'I think I could manage five or six.'

We laughed, and then worked in silence for a bit. I was wondering about Chloe's state of mind –

regarding Beast and Brendan in particular. I thought I'd do a little gentle probing.

'I saw Jess and Fred in the park last night.'

'You didn't say you'd been to the park!' Chloe sounded a tiny bit jealous.

'Oh, I just went for a stroll to clear my head. They're working for Major Events, you know – the same as Beast.'

I watched Chloe like a hawk. I knew I was playing with fire, here, mentioning such dangerous subjects. Unfortunately, her face was completely hidden by sunglasses, the wide khaki brim of her hat, and some handfuls of her wild red hair which had started to fall down. I couldn't tell if she was blushing or not.

'Lucky devils,' she said. 'Spending the whole summer organising parties. That's my kind of work.'

'It was so amazing of you to agree to work here instead,' I piled it on. 'But it might have been a bit weird working with Beast, anyway, mightn't it?'

'Weird?' said Chloe. 'Why?' She looked a tiny bit awkward.

'Well, what if he was turning on the charm with some new girl, right under your nose, or something?'

Chloe shrugged. 'Cool,' she said. 'No problem.' I hoped she was telling the hundred per cent truth, but I was still kind of in the dark.

'What did exactly happen between you and Beast, then?' I blurted out suddenly.

'Nothing,' said Chloe. 'And that's the truth. I got in a bit of a state about him, but I soon realised it was a total waste of time and he wasn't interested.' She didn't sound tragic, just brisk and matter-of-fact.

'Will you be OK if we run into him in Newquay?'

'Of course I will!' groaned Chloe. 'Why wouldn't I be?'

'He made you cry.'

'Zoe – loads of stuff makes me cry! Adverts with puppies make me cry – but I don't avoid watching them!'

'OK, OK.' I flapped my arms about to indicate defeat. 'Of course. Sorry.'

We went on weeding for ages. I was reassured about what she'd said about Beast. That guy was bad news and I didn't want Chloe to get hurt again.

'There was one thing about Beast,' said Chloe suddenly, 'that I didn't tell you.'

'What?' I demanded anxiously.

'Well, after he, like, made it clear he wasn't interested, uhhh . . . Well, I sent him a few stupid texts. Kind of . . . really stupid stuff, like, I was a bit of a love pest for a while, there. That's why I wanted to avoid him in the street that time. It wasn't cos I still fancy him or anything. It was because I'd been such a total idiot, all needy and gushing and . . . urrrrrgh! I can't bear the thought of those damn texts.'

'How did he react?'

'He ignored them for ages, then one day he just sent me a one-liner saying sorry, but I was on to a loser cos for some time he'd been mad about somebody else, and please not to send any more texts as his mum had accidentally seen one.'

'Oh God!'

'Yeah, cringe-making! And although when we met Beast in the street I felt fine, and I was even fine when he took me for coffee afterwards, you know, like, I was so over it, I was still just a tiny bit worried that he might be thinking of those freakin' texts, and maybe if I worked for Major Events he'd mention them one day or something, and I'd *die*. So maybe it was better for me to work on the farm after all.'

As she spoke, Brendan's Land Rover came rattling along the field's edge towards us.

'Hmmm,' murmured Chloe in my ear, 'and that's another great reason for working here. Hey! Shall we invite him to our picnic lunch? What do you think?'

I was in two minds. If we picnicked with Brendan, would we miss the chance of a lunch with Oliver in the farm kitchen?

'OK!' I whispered, 'Brendan today, Oliver tomorrow? Undo your top button; give him a glimpse of your divine freckles!'

Brendan was in our sights and the poor guy didn't know what was going to hit him. He got out of the Land Rover.

'Hi, Brendan!' Chloe grinned. 'We're going to have a picnic lunch today – want to join us? There's heaps!'

'Terrific idea!' said Brendan. 'Hop in! Oh, by the way, Zoe . . .' he added, looking mischievous, 'I've got a maggoty old ram in the back of the truck – he reminds me a bit of George Clooney. Take a look and tell me what you think!'

I went round the back of the Land Rover and peered in. It was Oliver!

CHAPTER 13

'Oh my God!' I yelped, covering up my mouth. 'Brendan told me you were a maggoty old ram!'

'Fair point,' said Oliver, smiling serenely. He knew he was gorgeous and would never be mistaken for a farm animal.

'We're going for a picnic lunch!' I grinned.

'I know,' said Oliver. 'I heard. Do you want to join me in First Class?' He held out his hand to haul me up. Oh my God! I was actually going to *touch* him! This was progress, by anybody's standards! I grabbed his hand (trying not to appear too desperate) and my insides turned a cute little somersault at his touch. His skin was cool and dry. I was glad. I would have had trouble with hot and sweaty. I would never wash my hand again, obviously. I clambered awkwardly up the back of the Land Rover and crashed down beside Oliver on a pile of filthy sacks.

For a split second I wished I had access to a mirror and some mascara. Three layers hardly seemed enough, now I was actually sitting right next to the love god. OK, it wasn't exactly marriage, but it was a start.

'It's the only way to travel!' I joked, as Brendan started the engine and we jolted back along the field towards the gate. I ransacked my brain for a magic sentence which would make Oliver love me for ever. Then I ransacked it again for any sentence at all. Then I tried to remember anything I had ever said. Just words. Any words. After about seven hours of howling silence, I took the plunge.

'Has your headache gone . . .' I blurted out suddenly, sounding disastrously like his mother, '. . . that you had yesterday?'

Oliver looked startled, then seemed to remember. 'Oh yeah, I'm fine today,' he replied.

'Oh good,' I said, deeply regretting ever having mentioned his headache. I waited for him to ask if my headache had gone, too, but he didn't. Disaster! He had forgotten that I'd ever had a headache! But I had not only remembered his, but been needy and nerdy enough to ask how he was.

Oh, cow poo of the vilest kind! My campaign to appear cool, unattainable and desirable had taken a disastrous dive.

There was nothing much I could do to increase my attractiveness. I could hardly slip into high heels and a figure-hugging little cocktail dress right now, so I just tried to lurch attractively whenever the Land Rover hit a rut. Oliver was totally silent, staring out towards the woods and trees. He was lost in his thoughts, which evidently did not include my former headache.

'Wonderful here, isn't it?' I sighed, and immediately regretted it.

'Mmm,' said Oliver. Oh God! He hadn't even awarded me a single word, only a kind of absent-minded hum! But I loved his silence in a way. It was better than being bombarded with sleazy chat-up lines by smooth-talking bigheads like Beast.

The Land Rover stopped and we got out – this time it was Brendan who gave me a hand down.

'So how's the head today, Zoe?' he asked. His concern was a startling contrast to Oliver's dreamy forgetfulness.

'Oh, fine, thanks, totally gone,' I said. 'It was just the polytunnel.'

'Well, that's grand.' Brendan grinned. Such lovely quaint Irish words! 'I happen to know that you won't be in the polytunnel this afternoon anyway – Martin's got something else lined up for you in the shade. I think Sarah gave him hell about you getting wet yesterday. I can tell when they've had a little set-to. There's a vibe.'

It was a perfect picnic spot: woods and hills on all sides, and totally silent except for the sound of a tinkling stream and the calls of birds and animals.

'Oh, it's magical!' said Chloe. Pigeons cooed from distant treetops, and the ewes and lambs bleated to one another nearby.

'Under this rowan tree, maybe,' said Brendan. I loved the way he knew the trees' names. We sat down under the tree beside the stream and unpacked our sandwiches. Oliver fished out a plastic box from his rucksack and opened it with a suspicious air.

'Who makes your packed lunch, Oliver?' asked Brendan. 'Your butler?'

Oliver looked faintly embarrassed. He didn't answer, just opened up a sandwich and glared at the ham and cheese within.

'I hate ham,' he said, and picked it out and flung it into a hedge.

'Hey!' quipped Brendan. 'I could have had that! The bottomless pit, that's me!'

Chloe laid out the sandwiches she had made: cheese and pickle, cucumber and tuna, and some jam sandwiches for herself.

'The tuna is for Zoe,' she warned Brendan sternly. 'So hands off!'

'Thanks so much, Chloe, this is fantastic!' I said, wondering if I could manage to take a huge bite of my sarnie while still looking moody and charismatic. 'Sarah's soup was kind of nice, but once I knew it had been bubbling away for months, it kind of lost its charm.'

'Cooking's not her strong point,' Brendan smiled, 'though Martin can do a mean chilli when he's in the mood.'

'What are Sarah and Martin like to live with?' I asked. 'You're staying in their house, right?'

'Oh, they're fine,' said Brendan. 'It's such a big old place, I've got most of the attic to myself and I've got my own TV up there and a bathroom and everything, so I just come and go as I please.'

The mention of bathrooms reminded me of the girl who had burst in yesterday while I was drying myself after the shower.

'What's Lily like?' I asked. 'I think I saw her briefly, yesterday? Petite with light brown hair in a ponytail?'

'Oh, that'll be Lily,' said Brendan, laughing. 'Trouble! She's broken every heart in Oxford – a brain the size of a planet, and spoilt rotten by her ma.' It sounded as if Brendan didn't rate her. I felt relieved for Chloe's sake.

'Does she ever work on the farm?'

'What! Lily! No, she'd never set foot out of doors if she could. She's a city girl. Although she does do the farmers' market stall sometimes – she likes to flirt with the customers.' He pulled a playful disgusted face.

It was obvious that, to make an impression on Brendan, Chloe had to present herself as the total opposite of Lily. But how was I supposed to make an impression on Oliver? He was staring out across the valley, looking kind of switched off.

'Do you fancy a game of pool some time, Oliver?' asked Brendan. 'There's a place in town, opposite the war memorial.'

'I don't really play pool,' said Oliver, looking tragic and picturesque. 'It doesn't really do it for me.'

'What does do it for you, then, Oliver?' Chloe

piped up, looking cheeky. 'What – or who?'

'I do a bit of running now and then,' said Oliver.

'Round the park?' asked Chloe, clearly trying to do a bit of research for my sake.

'No – I'm not crazy about the park,' he sighed, picking a stalk of grass and stroking his face with it. Lucky old stalk! I'd watch where he threw it afterwards, and if nobody was looking, I'd scoop it up into my pocket and keep it in a gold locket for ever.

'I love the park,' I said. OK, I adored Oliver, but I wasn't going to diss the dear old park for anybody. 'I met Jess Jordan and Fred Parsons there yesterday. They're working for Major Events – you know, the hospitality company. Chloe wanted to work there, but I twisted her arm.'

'Oh, you liked the idea of the farm?' queried Brendan, with a naughty twinkle in his eye. 'Why's that, then, Zoe?'

'I thought it sounded sweet and old-fashioned,' I said. 'But of course, now I realise I'm marooned with low-life yokels I'm deeply regretting my decision.'

Brendan and Chloe laughed, but Oliver only smiled slightly as if he hadn't really been listening properly.

'I can't stand Fred Parsons,' Oliver mused. 'He

thinks he's so damn funny, but he's really just weird and nerdy.' I was shocked. I've always liked Fred immensely, but somehow I didn't have the courage to say so now, and I hated myself for it.

'I love Fred!' exclaimed Chloe defiantly. Thank God. 'I think he's hilarious.'

'Well, they say a sense of humour is a very personal thing,' observed Brendan. 'But a sense of timing is crucial, and I have to tell you guys that it's ten to two, and if we don't get back to work, Martin will be emitting smoke.'

We started packing up. Oliver clambered to his feet and chucked his plastic box back into his rucksack without putting the lid on properly. A bit of lettuce fell into the bottom of the bag. This disturbed me slightly for some reason.

We drove back to the farmyard, Brendan and Oliver disappeared and Martin took us into a little shed where there were buckets of eggs, a set of scales and a vast bale of egg boxes. We spent the afternoon weighing and boxing up eggs into small, medium and large categories, while discussing how we were going to persuade our parents to let us go to Newquay alone.

I arrived home to find Tam back from hospital and

sorting out her room, while loud music throbbed from her speakers. When she saw me, she pulled me inside and shut the door. Then she placed her lips against my ear.

'Thanks so much for not saying anything yesterday!' she whispered, hugging me. 'I owe you, big time!'

'OK, OK.' I frowned. I was tired and I wanted peace and quiet and my own choice of music. Tam was going through a worrying rap phase.

'How's work? Is it OK? What's happening? Come out for a walk!' demanded Tam. 'I want to talk!'

CHAPTER 14

'Let's go out for half an hour!' insisted Tam. 'Twice round the park! I could do with some fresh air!'

'But I've been in the fresh air all day!' I wailed. It was no use. Tam switched off the music, grabbed me by the arm and practically frogmarched me downstairs. We peered into the sitting room. Mum and Dad were watching the news.

'We're going for a walk – two circuits of the park!' announced Tam. Mum looked up with a delighted smile. I knew what she was thinking. *Isn't it great that our beloved and distinguished older daughter, Tamsin, is such a good role model for that younger one – I forget her name – the one with the massive zit on her chin?*

'Dinner's at seven thirty!' she called. 'Dad's made aubergine parmigiana from Jamie Oliver's Italian book!'

Once we'd got out into the road, Tam's grip on my arm eased slightly and I was able to enjoy that underrated luxury: blood circulating freely to my fingertips.

'OK,' I said. 'Tell me about this Ed, then.'

'He's absolutely amazing!' sighed Tam.

'I know that already. How did you meet, again?'

'Well, you know Daisy from school, right? Her dad plays in this club cricket team, and there was a match on the Sunday, and Daisy wanted to go, so I tagged along, and guess what! Ed was the captain!' Tam couldn't have looked prouder if she'd fallen for the captain of England. 'We all had tea afterwards in the pavilion, and somehow I got talking to him, and Daisy was kind of wrapped up with some guy she's got a thing about – he's a radio astronomer, whatever that is – and Ed and I were kind of trapped in a corner of the pavilion together, and you know how it is, our eyes kind of met over the egg sandwiches.'

'So, what, you pulled right there and then under everybody's noses? Was his family there?'

'No, no, they were at the zoo or something. And it wasn't gross like that at all. He works with computers – so I had this brilliant excuse to ask his advice because it was Parv's birthday coming up. I was telling him about my birthday-present crisis and how Parv is fixated on electronic gadgets, and he told me he'd meet me at this brilliant shop in town and help me choose something.'

'Then what?' Despite my disapproval I was becoming horribly fascinated.

'Well, we met the next day in town and he showed me all the latest stuff, and we found a nice little thing for Parv, and then he took me out to lunch!' Her eyes shone.

We had reached the park, and I supposed that, to Tam, it must look fabulously romantic in the slanting evening sunlight. Personally, I was struggling with severe hunger and though Tam was deep in her erotic fantasy about Ed, I was already flirting passionately with the forthcoming aubergine parmigiana.

'By the time we'd finished our lunch I was totally under his spell, and he was, like, "You're the most beautiful woman I've ever *seen*," – and all that crap.' At least Tam had the grace to laugh off his compliments. 'And his foot kind of pursued my foot under the table and, well, from then on it was, like, totally magical. And the next day he took me out to lunch and drove me off into the country . . .'

'Where you had a Heathcliff and Cathy experience, I suppose?'

'Oh no, he's not Heathcliffish at all. He's totally civilised and, well, just amazing.'

'In the film of our lives, who would he be played by?' I demanded. The film of our lives has already been extensively cast. Tam is Kate Winslet, Dad is Simon Russell Beale, Mum is Harriet Walter or maybe Sophie Thompson, and for me it's most likely Danny DeVito, though when Chloe or Tam are trying to get round me they say it's Rachel Weisz.

'Oh . . . Ed would be . . . ahhh . . . Jude Law,' said Tam with a massive sigh.

'Wow!' I acknowledged, though I knew Tam's tendency to over-estimate her boyfriends' good looks. Ed might resemble Jude Law after a bad attack of chicken pox, for example.

'Tell me about his family,' I demanded. Tam winced.

'Oh, not much to tell,' she said hastily. 'Just – you know – dumb wife, two kids, the usual domestic trap.'

'She's dumb, huh?' I was determined to give Tam a hard time, now. I had slipped into Victorian Governess mode. 'Dumb for trusting him? For not realising he's messing about with you while she deals with the dirty nappies? What's her name?'

'Jo.' Tam winced again. 'The thing is, it's not her fault, but the magic's gone out of their marriage . . .'

'Of course the magic's gone out of her marriage!' I snapped. 'Because her lying dog of a husband is playing away!'

'Don't be horrid, Zoe,' said Tam, letting go of my arm and folding her hands defensively across her chest. 'I wish I hadn't told you now.'

'How old are the kids?' I persisted. 'What are their names?'

'I can't remember . . . they've got nicknames.'

'What are their nicknames?'

'Uhh . . . Little Bear and Twinkle.'

'Little Bear and Twinkle!' I exploded. 'I don't believe you! You're trying to steal Little Bear and Twinkle's daddy! How old are they? How old is *he*, for God's sake?'

'I'm not telling you any more! You're just totally negative all the time!'

'I'm just scared of what you're getting into!' I shouted. 'A horrible mess! Big trouble! Heartbreak all round!'

'Ed says he thinks she'd like an amicable separation, anyway,' said Tam huffily.

'What? Leaving her to look after two little kids all on her own? I don't think so!' I have babysat for the Norman twins, and I know what I'm talking about when it comes to the demands of childcare.

'They haven't had sex for months,' said Tam, looking guilty.

'So what? People with little kids never have sex, anyway.'

'Since when did you become such an expert on all this?'

'Angela Norman told me – when I arrived to babysit one day and she was covered with sick. She said, "God, Zoe, having toddlers doesn't do anything for your love life. I don't think we've even kissed since Christmas." And that was in May.'

'Well, I don't think Ed and his wife are suited anyway. He says she doesn't understand him.'

'Oh, Tam! They all say that! It's the cheating husband's cliché! I was reading about it in an agony column only the other day!' I wailed in exasperation. I was so cross that Tam just couldn't see it. '*My wife doesn't understand me* . . . Utter crap!'

Suddenly we heard pounding feet behind us. The park is full of joggers and you have to be prepared to give way to them. We turned round and stood aside.

But when he saw us, the jogger thundered to a halt. It was Beast.

'Tam! And the lovely Zoe!' He grinned. 'Wow! Jackpot! Tam! Haven't seen you since Easter – come here, you fabulous temptress!' And he swept her into his arms. I stood there like a plank, staring at the daisies. Not that I wanted him to give me a hug, of course. I wouldn't want to hug him if he was the last guy on earth. I knew what he was like. In ten years' time he was going to be whispering to some poor deluded girl, 'My wife doesn't understand me.' I'm sorry, but as far I was concerned, men like Beast and Ed were the scum of the earth.

CHAPTER 15

'Hi, Zoe!' Beast beamed, emerging from his hug with Tam. 'Don't worry, I'm not going to hug you. Zoe disapproves of me, big time.' He cracked a feral grin at Tam.

'Join the club!' exclaimed Tam. 'She was just telling me what a total idiot I am, when you arrived to rescue me.'

'Let's be idiots together,' said Beast, throwing his arm around Tam's shoulder. It was annoying of them. Tam kind of snuggled up to him and pulled a face at me – the face of a rebellious toddler who has found a big strong ally.

'So how's the job at the farm going?' Beast asked me breezily, as we resumed our walk.

'It's OK.' I shrugged.

'And what about the Newquay plan?' Beast went on. 'Found somewhere to stay yet?'

'Well, the Newquay plan is still active,' I admitted. 'But we haven't found anywhere to stay, and loads of places seem to have a rule about no under-eighteens. I think we'll probably join Flora in Tuscany.' I didn't want to say that my mum had forbidden me to go. It would make me sound like a goddam baby. 'How's Major Events? Fred and Jess work for them, too, don't they?'

Beast started on the subject of the hospitality business, and Tam was predictably impressed, which left me to slouch along beside them looking at the path and thinking of Little Bear and Twinkle. God, how I wished those kids were called something really pretentious like Panache or Dillinger.

I tried to think who would play Beast in the movie of our lives. It had to be Joaquin Phoenix.

When we reached the bandstand, I had a sudden urge to go back home. Beast and Tam were having so much fun together and I just felt like an outsider.

'I'm going home, Tam,' I said. 'I'm starving. I was starving when I came home and you just marched me straight out again and if I don't have something now, I'll faint.'

'Poor little Zoe!' said Beast. 'Tam, you're a bully. Here, babe.' He pulled a bar of chocolate out of his pocket. It was the hazelnut sort – my favourite. I was determined to refuse, though. After all, he was the dreaded, the hated, the manipulative, the chauvinistic Beast. He tore off the wrapper, broke off a huge chunk, and held it out to me.

I backed off. 'Sorry,' I muttered. 'Thanks, but . . .' I wanted that choccy so badly. 'I can't – I'm allergic to chocolate.'

'She's not allergic to chocolate!' Tam grinned. 'She's just on one of her doomed diets, I expect.'

The bitch! My 'doomed diets', eh? I felt myself explode inside. My prize zit, Nigel, throbbed away evilly. My face must have been the colour of plum crumble. Beast still held out the chocolate.

'Go on, babe,' he said. 'You don't need to diet – you're perfect as you are!' And he cocked his head on one side and winked at me.

Somehow this only made me more furious. I just turned and ran off. Luckily I was still wearing my old trainers (because of the farm), so I could run fast – well, by my knock-kneed and slightly podgy standards.

'Zoe!' I heard Tam wail. 'Come back! Don't be a prat!'

I accelerated away. I knew Beast could catch me just like that if he wanted to. But I guessed he wouldn't try. He evidently thought of me as trouble and he was the kind of guy who would do anything for a quiet life. Actually, I hate rows, which is why I felt such a heavy sense of approaching doom about Tam and her secret thing with Ed, and poor Little Bear and Twinkle. It just couldn't end happily. No matter how devoted and gorgeous and Jude Law-like he was, no matter how tired and irritable his wife was, he had Little Bear and Twinkle waiting for him at home. How could he ever love Tam more than them? I practically loved them more than her already, and I hadn't even met them.

But seriously . . . I do so adore Tam, and the thought of her getting hurt was just utterly sick-making. Once out of the park, I slowed to a walk and whipped out my mobile. I called Toby.

'Tobe!' I wailed. 'Life is spiralling out of control! And I can't bear it cos I'm a control freak!'

'But, darling!' cried Tobe in his Noel Coward voice. 'That in itself is terribly terribly attractive, you know!'

'What are you doing, Tobe?' I enquired. 'Any news on the love front? What about Maria at the Dolphin?'

'She's gone off me now, dear,' confided Toby. 'Because I dropped a tray of glasses and loads of them smashed. She called me a cack-handed nitwit – but I'm sure she meant it as a compliment!' He giggled. I love Tobe. He always makes me feel better.

'Toby, promise me one thing – if nobody else wants us by the time we're thirty, will you marry me?'

'Try to stop me, lover! Although I might have to marry Ferg as well. Nothing kinky. We can have a celibate ménage à trois!'

'Brilliant idea!' I grinned. 'Regard yourself as booked!'

I arrived home sweatily unattractive, but feeling slightly less stressy. I kicked off my trainers and ran upstairs for a shower. Dad called up from the kitchen door.

'Supper in ten!'

Dear Dad. He would never dream of abandoning his irritating wife and revolting daughters to frolic with a much younger woman. At least, I hope not. The shower was the best moment of the day so far. I basked in a deluge of jasmine-scented foam.

Moments later, there was a tap on the door. Presumably Tam coming to apologise – or even refuse to apologise. Couldn't I have a moment of peace even in the bathroom, for God's sake? I ignored the knock and continued to dry myself (one of the most boring jobs on earth, incidentally).

'Zoe?' Oh no. It was Mum. Wondering where her beloved Tam was, no doubt. 'Zoe!'

'What!? I'm just getting dressed.'

'Toby rang just now and left a message.'

'Oh – what?' Damn! I hate it when Tobe rings me on the landline. I must have left my mobile in my rucksack down in the hall.

'Well, the message was that he forgot to say he'd found somewhere for you all to stay in Newquay, but Dad was the one who answered the phone, otherwise I'd have let him know in no uncertain terms that this Newquay plan is just *not on*, Zoe – at least as far as you're concerned!'

CHAPTER 16

It's hard to storm out in a rage when you're naked. But at least my overwhelming surge of fury and indignation would help the drying process. I heard Mum hesitate, waiting for my inevitable yelling. I did not yell. I would rather plan a really cold, cutting, seething, searing speech and deliver it fully dressed, in five minutes' time.

'Zoe,' she said after a few seconds, 'did you hear me?'

I remained silent, accumulating points for coolness under fire – in my own eyes, anyway. Then I heard Mum give a kind of exasperated groan and slip away downstairs. I was so enraged at her attitude, I felt full of white-hot fire – as if I'd swallowed a whole barbecue. I finished drying myself, combed my hair, dived into a dressing gown and marched into my bedroom.

I selected one of my long dark dramatic dresses and heavy silver earrings – the sort a Greek goddess might have worn when confronting her demons. I applied fearsome scarlet lipstick. A pair of high heels completed the picture. OK, I'd have to go downstairs really carefully – a stumble and headlong dive would not be the entrance I was planning. With my killer heels on, I'd be able to look down on Mum, because though ferocious, she is only five foot four inches whereas I am five foot six, and with my heels, five foot ten.

I stalked downstairs and strode into the kitchen. Mum was pouring out glasses of wine. Tam was back from the park and sitting at the table. Dad was creating a salad at the far end of the kitchen. My face must have been contorted with rage, because they all looked at me and cringed with a kind of spineless dread. Synchronised cringing is a major sport in our house. If only it was an Olympic event we'd have gold medals wall-to-wall.

'Right!' I snapped, glaring at Mum. 'I've had enough of all this about not going to Newquay. There's no possible reason I can't go. Everybody's going. The only reason I'm doing this poxy job is so I can save up enough money to pay for it.'

'It's not as simple as that,' said Mum, gritting her teeth. Much of her professional life is spent arguing so I knew I was in for a big battle. 'It's our job as parents to look after your welfare, and we would be neglecting our duty if we let you go.'

'Go ahead!' I snapped. 'Neglect your duty! All the other parents think it's cool. Chloe's going. Toby's going. Fergus is going. And so am I – whether you like it or not.'

'You are *not* going!' Mum's voice rose and her eyes flashed.

'I *am* going!' I shouted, flashing my eyes right back.

Dad flinched and headed for the garden. 'Herbs . . .' he muttered, 'for the salad . . .' And he darted out. The sap!

'You won't get your way by shouting at me, Zoe!' Mum's voice had taken on a soaring, laser-like acidic quality. If there had been milk on the table, it would have curdled.

'I'm *going*!' I yelled.

Glasses on the dresser rattled slightly. Tam scrambled to her feet and ran away upstairs. I was just furious that Tam and Dad, who should have been supporting me, had sneakily run off to get out of the firing line. If I'd wanted to, I could have dished the dirt on Tam and totally wrecked her summer. But I'd supported her and kept quiet. Why couldn't she support me? Still, I couldn't be bothered to think of her right now. I was totally fixed and focused on one thing: my hol in Newquay.

'Zoe! We've discussed this and you know my views! It's no use you just assuming that things will happen because you want them to! It's out of the question!'

'When Dad was fourteen,' I dropped my voice to a low, buzzing, menacing snarl, 'he went off to the Forest of Dean with his mate Tony – camping. On their own! And they were only fourteen!'

'Dad was a boy!' cried Mum. 'It was the 1970s! Things were different then! And it's different for girls! Men prey on girls! There are so many dreadful things that could happen!'

'Nothing bad is going to happen in Newquay!' I screamed. 'Why do you always stop me from doing the most harmless ordinary things? You're always on my case! Tam is allowed to do anything and I'm never allowed even to leave the house for a split second without you having a nervous breakdown!' I may have been exaggerating slightly here, but what the hell, it felt great.

At this point, the front doorbell rang. There was a moment's silence. I had a sudden feeling it would be Toby. He does sometimes drop round in the evening if he's on the way to the leisure centre. I decided if it was Tobe, I'd just leave the house as I was, wet hair and high heels and everything, and go with him to the leisure centre, to the ends of the earth, anywhere. Just to be out of this hellhole.

'I'll get it,' I snapped, and marched out of the kitchen. I could see a shadow waiting, through the glass. Maybe it was the dreaded axe-murderer. He'd decided he couldn't wait to axe me on the sands at Newquay – he was going to axe me right here on my own doorstep. Well, that was OK by me. My blood sugar was now so low (caused by prolonged starvation and horrible shouting) that the axe-murderer would have been welcome. I flung the door open. Astonishment! It was Beast.

He took in my appearance: the long black dress, the supernatural earrings, the killer heels, the killer face – and kind of winced.

'Tam's upstairs,' I said. 'I'll call her.'

'No!' said Beast. 'Wait! It's you I wanted a word with, Zoe. Come out here a minute.'

He beckoned me down my own garden path. Impatiently I stalked down the path and took up what I hoped was a cool and aggressive slouch against the gatepost, with my arms folded.

'You look amazing,' said Beast, running his eyes up and down my fabulous black number.

'You shouldn't look people up and down like that,' I snapped. 'It's not polite.' Beast kind of flared his eyes, looked surprised, looked thoughtful, and smiled sort of privately to himself, which only stoked up my blazing fury even more. 'Anyway,' I went on, 'get on with it, because my supper's on the table and I'm in the middle of a particularly enjoyable row with my mum.'

I was so, so hungry, and so angry, I could have fainted out of sheer spite. I didn't have time for this.

'I was going to ask you if you'd like to come out for a drink sometime,' said Beast, looking me in the eye, suddenly very bold and direct. His eyes were huge and dark and kind of hypnotising.

'What?' I gasped in amazement.

'Just a drink one night,' said Beast. 'That new bar in the high street is fantastic. If you're too tired in the week we could go on Saturday.'

'What? What?' I was speechless.

'I'm asking you out,' said Beast. 'I think you're terrific, a legend, and I've wanted to ask you for ages.'

'I don't believe you!' I gasped. 'How could I even consider it, after all that stuff with you and Chloe?'

'Hey! Hey! Steady on!' protested Beast, with an argumentative-but-charming smile, 'There never was *stuff* between me and her. I admit I did have a little cuddle with her in the back of the car on the way home once, but that was only because I'd had a bit too much to drink – I apologised for it later, like a gentleman.'

'Well, you asked her to the sixth-form dance and when she got there she realised you'd asked another girl as well!' I still felt angry with Beast for being so insensitive towards Chloe, even though she'd admitted to me that it had been just a crush on her part, and she'd been the once nuisance-texting.

'No! Wait!' protested Beast. 'Listen! I didn't ask her: I asked you both. I didn't have anybody special lined up.'

'And isn't that just like you!' I hissed. 'You've got absolutely no conscience whatever. You'll just grab the nearest girl – no matter who – and if somebody else thought she was special, hard luck.' I sort of knew I might be being a bit hard on Beast, but I couldn't help it: the row with Mum was still blazing in my veins and a kind of general fury had taken me over.

'You're talking crap, babe,' said Beast hastily. He dropped his voice. 'I asked you both to that dance hoping that *you* would come. Because it's you I think about all the time. You're the one who's special. Not Chloe, not Sharon or whoever was clinging on to my arm at the sixth-form thing. I even forget who it was. I was so gutted you hadn't turned up. So listen, Zoe – please, please, sweetheart, can we put all this behind us and start again?'

'No, we freakin' well can't!' I was so astonished by what he'd said, I'd gone all weak and trembly. 'Don't you realise I really despise the way you behave? Flirting and groping and drooling over every girl in sight? I'm sick to death of men who play around. You never know where you are with them – they just ignore their responsibilities and grab whoever they fancy . . .' (I was thinking of Little Bear and Twinkle, here, to be honest, but I was sure that in ten years' time, Beast would be behaving just like Ed.)

'You've got me all wrong, babe . . .' Beast tried to protest. 'You're the only –'

'Shut up!' I snapped. 'I've had enough! I wouldn't go out with you if you were *the last guy left alive*!'

For a split second Beast didn't seem able to conjure up any kind of smile at all. I just whirled round on my killer heels and stalked back up the path. It should have been a great moment, actually, but I had the silliest feeling that the moment I was in private I was going to burst into tears.

CHAPTER 17

'Who was that?' said Mum suspiciously. 'Was it Toby?'

'No, no, no!' I snapped.

'Who was it, then?'

'Nobody. Nothing.'

Dad was bringing the aubergine parmigiana to the table. It smelt superb, but my brain was jarred. I tried to tune back into the row I'd been having with Mum, but Beast's visit had been so distracting, I couldn't think of anything else for a moment. Why on earth would he do such a thing? When he knew I disapproved of him? Was it all some kind of tasteless charade? Was he just trying to humiliate me? If I'd agreed to the date, I bet he wouldn't have showed up, and left me hanging about looking like a lemon. Why?

Was it revenge for my disapproval of him and Chloe?

'Zoe? Anything wrong, old boy? Dinner too salty or something?' Dad's anxious face bobbed into my vision. I shook myself back into the here and now.

'It's delicious, Dad,' I assured him. It was, too. But somehow I had so little appetite, it might as well have been cardboard. I kept on chewing. You don't really need to chew aubergine parmigiana all that much, actually: it's a bit like lasagne, kind of baby food for grown-ups. But I was having trouble getting every mouthful down.

'Now, regarding this wretched holiday row which keeps grumbling on,' said Mum, 'we've got to get things sorted and clear the air. We're planning a week away at the end of August . . .'

'Sorry, but I'm not coming,' I said. I didn't mention Newquay, though I knew it was all part of Mum's cunning plan to get me to abandon it.

'You don't even know where we're going yet,' said Mum coaxingly.

'Where are you going, then?' I sighed. Mum looked shifty.

'We're not sure yet,' she said. 'Somewhere nice. You can help us decide. You might be able to come, too, Tam.'

Tam looked startled and anxious.

'Oh – actually,' she said, 'normally I'd love to come with you guys and stuff, but I've promised Parv that I'll go up and see her at the end of August.' I knew that was a lie. She wanted to stay here while Mum and Dad were away, so she could have naughty lunches out in the country with her precious Ed while Little Bear and Twinkle waited tearfully for Daddy to come back home.

I gave Tam a hard, aggressive stare. She looked away, trying to appear normal. A horrid pang of heartburn went soaring up my throat. Indigestion! Or possibly a heart attack? OK, I was a tad young for a coronary, but they do say stress is the worst factor. And I had certainly never been so stressed out in my entire life. I put down my knife and fork and started sipping water. Dad noticed right away.

'Are you OK, old boy?' he enquired. 'I hope I haven't accidentally poisoned you.'

'No, Dad,' I sighed, massaging my tummy. 'The dinner's lovely. It's just all this aggravation.'

Dad looked sympathetic. Mum was glaring at me.

'Do you want an indigestion pill?' she demanded, getting up and going to the dresser. I didn't like her tone. When Tam had been laid low by her 'appendicitis' Mum had been tender and loving. With me, it was Throw It A Pill. She offered me one of those peppermint-and-chalk things that taste revolting.

'No, thanks,' I said. 'I think I'll go to my room. Excuse me.' Politeness, when icy, can be more insulting than rudeness. I hoped so anyway.

I went upstairs and instantly called Toby on my moby. Normally I'd have enjoyed that little rhyme, but today my mood was so black, nothing was going to cheer me up.

'Tobe!' I cried. 'My mum still says I can't come!'

'Don't give up,' urged Toby. 'It took me three weeks to convince my mum.'

'I'll never convince her,' I sighed bitterly. 'I might just have to run away. What's this place you've found?' I was even more desperate for details of Newquay now that it was forbidden fruit.

'Well, Fergus's cousin Gary, right? He's got a mate, and his mate's uncle's got a garage on the road into Newquay, and there's a bit of rough ground out the back, and he says we can camp there. It's right next to the loos, so that'll be – uh – convenient.'

'What?!' I gasped in disgust. This sounded about as manky as accommodation has ever been. Fergus's cousin Gary is a famously sordid person, but I was amazed that even he had thought that camping on some rough ground next to some public loos behind a garage might be a good idea. 'Toby, I'm sorry, but it sounds grotesque! For a minute I'm almost relieved my mum has said I can't go!'

'Hmmm . . . I'm slightly glad you've said that, actually,' admitted Toby. 'I was wondering how I could survive without a daily shower. But it is free.'

'So is getting run over!' I reminded him. 'And the reason it's free is that nobody in their right mind would camp there even if they were being paid.'

'That's a bit harsh,' said Toby. 'You haven't even seen it.'

'Toby, I can imagine exactly what it's like,' I said. 'I bet there are rusting old cars everywhere . . .'

'Not many, apparently,' said Toby sounding furtive.

'And rats.'

'I shouldn't think so.'

'But anyway, Tobe, Fergus's cousin Gary is a sleaze ball. I just know that this uncle's garage will be covered in girlie calendars, pools of oil and leering mechanics. It's just not the sort of place you'd want to take a lady.'

'You're right,' said Toby. 'I'm almost too ladylike

for it myself. But I might have to go, if Fergus puts his tiny foot down. What about you, though?'

'My mum will change her mind,' I promised him firmly. 'Or I'm leaving home.'

'Oh,' said Toby. 'OK, then. If you want to leave home right away, you can live in my garden shed with my hamsters, if you like. I'll put out a saucer of bread and milk for you every night.' I promised that, were I to become homeless, Toby's hamsters would have a new room-mate. But I was hoping it wouldn't come to that. My mum might yet weaken and capitulate. I might manage to slip a surrendering kind of herb into her tea.

'I'm going to get my dad to work on her,' I told him. 'Listen – the thought of a week in Newquay is the only thing that's keeping me going.'

We agreed that if Newquay was impossible, a suicide pact might become necessary, though we couldn't agree on the means. I wanted as violent a death as possible, involving a ski lift, a speed boat, a helicopter and a shoal of piranha fish, but Tobe just wanted to pass away peacefully in his bed from an overdose of marshmallows.

I rang off feeling a little better, though it's a sign of how bad things have got if you're cheered up by a conversation about stylish ways to end it all.

There was a tap on the door and Tam peeped round. She looked furtive.

'Are you OK?' she whispered. 'Can I come in?' I made room for her on the bed. 'It's a nightmare, this plan of Mum's for a family hol,' she said. 'But I'm sure we can crack it. Mum's downstairs watching *French and Saunders*. Dad's in his study. We've got to get him on our side.'

'How are we supposed to do that?' I asked with a sigh. My brain felt slow and frazzled. Tam was going to have to do all the thinking.

'We've got to make him realise how much more wonderful and romantic it would be if it was just him and Mum having a lovely little holiday, a kind of second honeymoon, just the two of them, with candle-lit dinners and lots of old churches and stuff. Let's corner him in his study,' whispered Tam. 'We've got to do a big matchmaking act – with our own parents.'

'Yuck,' I murmured as we tiptoed across the landing to Dad's door. 'Gross!'

CHAPTER 18

We crept into Dad's room. He was listening to Queen as usual – Dad always has this on when he's stuck with his work designing scientific websites. He sat staring at his computer screen and thoughtfully cradling a glass of red wine. Tam wrapped her arms around his neck. I sat on the floor, rested my head on his knee and played with his shoelaces. This has been my favourite trick since I was three.

'No, you can't have any money,' said Dad playfully.

'Money!' exclaimed Tam. 'Don't be so vulgar. Money's not an issue. Zoe's got a job, and I've been slaving away at the Turk's Head for more than a month – or haven't you noticed?'

'We think you and Mum deserve a holiday on your own,' I said, removing his shoe and giving him a foot massage. 'Think how romantic it would be, just you and Mum together, like when you were students.'

'Romantic candlelit dinners,' sighed Tam, playing with his hair. 'Hours and hours in museums without us getting all bored and tetchy.'

'No horrid teenager demanding to leave the art gallery instantly in order to flog round boutiques for hours on end,' I added, stroking his ankles.

'Look,' said Dad, putting down his wine and rubbing his nose thoughtfully. Nose-rubbing is always a sign that somebody has reservations about something – well, you can't imagine somebody saying 'Marry me, I love you madly' while rubbing their nose, can you? I'm thinking of reading body language at uni.

'I know you two have got other fish to fry at the end of August,' Dad went on. 'God knows what you're planning and, frankly, if it was up to me, I'd just let you get on with it, as long as I didn't have to know anything about it.'

'Yes,' crooned Tam, playing with his ears. 'That shows what a fabulous dad you are.'

'No,' said Dad. 'It shows what an irresponsible selfish prat I am, actually – though of course, if anybody ever even dreamed of hurting either of you,

I would kill them with my bare hands.'

Tam and I exchanged a look, but we managed not to laugh. The idea of Dad killing anything with his bare hands is a joke. He has a crisis of conscience even if you ask him to swat a wasp.

'But Mum's trip isn't booked yet,' he went on. 'Anything could happen to stop it.'

'But we don't want you *not* to have a hol, Dadda!' cried Tam, stroking his hair. 'You and Mum must go away and chill and have quality time all to yourselves. Away from the hurly-burly of us.'

'Yeah, right,' I sighed. 'Tam's the nearest thing to Liz Hurley available locally, and I'm as burly as can be!' I was beginning to feel better. Dad's attitude to Mum's holiday plans was encouraging. He plainly wasn't exactly gagging for us all to be trapped on holiday together.

'To be honest,' he said, 'I think she might like the idea of just the two of us going walking in North Wales.'

'Yes, yes!' said Tam. 'Think of the lovely ferns and rocks and little tea rooms.'

'That reminds me,' I interrupted, 'supper was delicious. I just couldn't eat because I was fed up with everybody. I'll go down and heat a bit up in the microwave in a minute.' Dad looked pleased. I think he's touched that I have inherited his greed.

'So,' said Tam, 'do a Google search on romantic B&Bs in Snowdonia – or cosy cottages with log fires and beams.'

'I'll run it past the boss,' said Dad, smiling.

'Great!' Tam grinned, and kissed the top of his head. 'Just don't tell her we had this conversation.'

'What conversation?' Dad shrugged theatrically and placed his finger on his lips. He was definitely on our side. The trouble is, he's so easy-going. His idea of standing up to Mum is lying down and letting her drive over him – in a tank. In their previous lives, he was a harmless vole and she was a boa constrictor.

Next morning I met Chloe at the bus stop as usual. I couldn't wait to confide all the ghastly details of the previous evening. Not the bit about Beast asking me out, though. That was top of my list of Things to Hide from Chloe. What if I told her he'd tried to hit on me, and she was still secretly crazy about him? She'd go ballistic. I had the feeling I didn't want to discuss Beast with Chloe ever again. It was all becoming so tormented.

'Hey, Zoe, mega-disaster!' She grabbed me, her

eyes blazing with melodrama. 'I spent hours online yesterday looking for places to stay in Newquay, and there's literally zilch! All the caravan sites really are for couples and families only. I looked at hundreds of places.'

'Well, that's the least of our problems,' I told her. 'My mum's still adamant that I can't go at all. What about your mum?'

'My mum was OK about it,' said Chloe. 'She said she thought we'd be all right as long as we stuck together. I had to solemnly swear I wouldn't drink, though.'

'God! Your mum is so great!' I sighed enviously. 'I have to think of a way to get mine on board. She's threatening to take me and Tam away on a horrendous family hol, now.'

Chloe looked anxious, because her mum's permission clearly depended on our being in Newquay together, joined at the hip and drinking only lemonade. We were a bit quiet on the bus, and later in the field, we worked separately, lost in our thoughts. I had so many issues, I couldn't hold it all in my head at once: Mum's stupid strictness, Tam's secret adultery, Beast's astonishing visit last night . . .

'Newquay looks even more fabulous than I

thought it would,' sighed Chloe as we approached lunchtime. 'God! There's clubs and bowling and gyms and aerobics studios and swimming pools with flumes and . . . oh God, if only we were old enough to stay at Blue Flash Surf Lodge! They've got a late-licensed seventies retro bar and everything! But it's over-eighteens only . . .'

'Even if it was under-eighteens,' I reminded her, 'my mum won't let me go. I think I may have to leave home. Toby's already offered me accommodation in his garden shed.'

I told Chloe about Toby and Fergus's plan to camp behind the garage. She wasn't as disgusted as I'd have expected.

'I don't know, Zoe,' she said. 'It might be OK . . . Have you got a tent? It might be OK as a last resort.'

'Chloe,' I said patiently, 'did you not hear what I said? My mum won't let me go.'

Chloe sat back on her heels and stared soberly at me for a minute. Then she thoughtfully picked her nose and flicked the bogey away across the rows of carrots.

'Oh God, Zoe,' she said. 'What are we going to do? And I've just persuaded my mum and every-thing . . .'

She stared dismally away towards a clump of trees. Suddenly an ice-cold thought entered my brain like a dagger. What if Chloe decided to go with Toby and Fergus and leave me behind? My imagination went into horror overdrive. This was the worst nightmare scenario so far.

CHAPTER 19

I was just planning to run away from home and not speak to my mum again for five years when the Land Rover arrived, with Brendan driving and Oliver sitting in the passenger seat. I was still reeling from the idea that Chloe might go to Newquay without me, so for once I hardly registered Oliver's presence.

'Hop in, girls!' He grinned. 'Who's for a picnic? I've brought a few bits and pieces myself this time, and as it's clouding over I thought we could have it in the hay barn.'

Oliver jumped out and helped me into the back again, while Chloe jumped into the cab alongside Brendan. I was still scared in case she had started to plan a trip to Newquay without me, but I was a hundred per cent behind her in her attempt to pull Brendan. He was such a lovely bloke.

When we got to the barn, the guys helped us up on to the huge pile of bales. Oliver's hand was warmer today. I had held hands with him twice now! Maybe, if I made sure that every day involved some climbing, I could hold his hand every day for the next month. What a shame we weren't working in the Himalayas.

I'd brought some French bread, hummus and satsumas; Chloe had some ham sandwiches and olives; and Brendan produced some pepperoni and spring onions. Oliver had fruit again, and a packet of crisps – smoky bacon. So that was his favourite! I planned to rub a few smoky bacon crisps on to my pulse points next time we were due to meet.

'I'm not sure about spring onions,' said Chloe nervously. 'They make your breath smell.'

'Well, you'll be all right,' promised Brendan with a naughty smile, 'as long as you're not planning on kissing anybody. Zoe, would you like one?'

'No thanks,' I said. 'They're a bit strong.'

'So you're planning on kissing somebody?' twinkled Brendan.

'No way!' I grinned, blushing. I didn't look

anywhere near Oliver. I didn't even look at his boots.

Chloe had prepared jam sandwiches for herself as usual, and brought a little Munch Bunch yogurt.

'What's with all this nursery food, Chloe?' asked Brendan. 'Jam sandwiches again?'

'I have to eat jam sandwiches every day,' said Chloe nervously. 'I'm hypo-allergenic.'

I wasn't sure this was the right word. Brendan raised his eyebrows.

'I'm interested in wild food,' he said. 'Nettle soup, that kind of thing.'

Chloe pulled a disgusted face. I started to worry that Chloe's food fads would put Brendan off. I would have to force her to swallow a whole oak tree in front of him – that should do the trick.

'Oh, I nearly forgot!' He smiled. 'I picked some fresh watercress just now, down in the stream. Here . . .' He reached inside his rucksack and brought out a rather muddy carrier bag.

'Has that been washed?' asked Oliver suspiciously, peering at it.

'It's been washed in the stream!' Brendan assured him. 'Its whole life has been one continuous rinsing.'

Chloe backed off – even sitting down, she can refuse food in a way which is almost acrobatic. And

Oliver shook his head sadly, as if the watercress was a big mistake.

Brendan was cramming it into his mouth and crunching away and saying how wonderful and peppery it was.

'What about liver fluke?' asked Oliver.

'What's liver fluke?' asked Chloe.

'It's an interesting disease,' said Oliver. 'It's a parasite called *Fasciola hepatica* which has two hosts. First it parasitises a snail, then it moves on to cattle, sheep, or humans. It attacks the liver.'

'Ugh!' shrieked Chloe.

'It's no picnic.' Oliver shook his head doubtfully.

'You're wrong there, Olly!' grinned Brendan, still chewing. 'A picnic is precisely what it is! My picnic!'

Brendan was so obviously trying to make Oliver look like a big girl's blouse with his macho gobbling of dangerous wild food. But I found Oliver's quiet scientific manner a turn-on. I so loved it when he talked Latin! We would call our first son Caesar!

At this moment my phone rang. 'Hello, old boy! How's agriculture?' It was Dad. This could only mean one thing. He must have persuaded Mum to let me go to Newquay. I crawled away into a semi-private corner of the hayloft.

'Listen, Zoe, I've had a brilliant idea,' said Dad. 'We could *all* go to Newquay! Together! *En famille*!'

My heart plummeted violently through the bales of hay and the rocks beneath until it arrived at the molten centre of the earth. 'I haven't actually run it past the boss,' Dad prattled on, 'but it could be the answer! We would rent a cottage somewhere, and you and Chloe could share a room. There's loads of interesting things down there – I'd no idea. I've been surfing the websites. There's a thing called the Saints Trail – you know how Mum loves walking – and loads of wonderful old houses and gardens – there's even a Japanese garden and bonsai nursery – and the history is fantastic! The history of pilchard fishing and mining, and sacred sites, not to mention King Arthur's castle just down the coast.'

I was drowning in the shock and horror. To think that only a moment earlier I had been stressing out over eating a few leaves of watercress! Now I was prepared to eat whole streams full of watercress, complete with slugs, leeches and live trout, if I could only escape from the threatening horror of a family holiday to Newquay.

I could imagine it in vivid, toe-curling detail. *Oh, hey, guys, sorry I can't come surfing today but we're going on a seven-mile walk with my mum and dad to visit the ruins of the pilchard mines and after that Mum wants to visit the Bonsai monastery.*

What could be worse? Apart from one's parents actually plunging eagerly into the surf themselves, and tagging along when night fell and we wanted to go clubbing.

'Dad . . .' It was so hard to say this. 'It's really kind of you to think of this . . .'

'Kind?' exploded Dad. 'It would be a treat for me, old boy! I wonder if they do wetsuits in my size?'

At the thought of this horror I almost literally retched. 'We'll have to talk about this when I get home,' I said. 'I can't talk now, sorry.'

'Oh, are you working?' asked Dad. 'Sorry. I thought you'd be on your lunch break. I was just so excited when I thought of it, I had to tell you right away.'

'Talk when I get home, right?' I said, briskly terminating the conversation.

I rang off and turned round. Oliver was lying on his back and staring at the roof of the barn, but Brendan was *actually holding Chloe's hand*!

CHAPTER 20

'Look, something's bitten me, Zoe!' Chloe held out her hand. 'Brendan thinks it's a sort of little insect that lives in the hay.' I looked at her hand with its tiny red swelling.

'Hmm, could be fatal,' I suggested. 'Maybe we should get out of this barn and go back to town, where we belong.'

'Oh no, Zoe!' giggled Chloe. 'I lurve the country-side! Anyway there's loads of pests in town. I could live in this barn. Hey! Do you think Martin and Sarah would let us spend the night here?' She turned to Brendan, and her eyes were very, very shiny in that tell-tale way which has to do with trying to sweep a guy off his feet.

Brendan looked dubious. 'Ah, there'd be loads of

little creatures biting you all night,' he said, shaking his head.

'You could protect us!' Chloe grinned. 'Or be on hand to administer first aid! You come too, Oliver!'

Oliver shook his head. 'I'm not brilliant in this kind of environment,' he said. 'Because of hay fever.'

'And you're not going to get me away from my attic,' said Brendan. 'After I've been working out of doors all day the last thing I want to do is have fleas and rats jumping over me all night.'

Chloe screamed. I had to admire the way Brendan had got out of this tight corner. And I also had to admire the way, if Chloe fancied a guy, she'd find some excuse to spend the night with him without it looking too saucy.

'I don't fancy it either,' I said. 'Things that are lovely in the daylight have a way of going sinister after dark.'

Oliver gave me a look for a split second, and my insides did another of those secret somersaults. It was as if we shared a moment of understanding. I'm not sure quite what we were understanding, though. It might have been that I was way more intriguing and desirable than my crazy friend. It may just have been that he had forgotten my name.

When I got home that night, Dad came hurtling out of the kitchen and hustled me into the dining room.

'I'm doing Jamie's fish-with-olives dish!' he whispered. 'That'll get her in the mood for Newquay!' Then he remembered some little cookery thing he needed to do and dashed off back to the kitchen.

I ran upstairs. I had to discuss the crisis with Tam. She was sitting on the floor of her room surrounded by lingerie.

'Shut the door!' she whispered. I obeyed, and then sat on the bed.

'Dad's got this terrible idea about us all going to Newquay!' I warned her. 'We've got to head him off and make him see it would literally be the most appalling holiday in history.'

'Never mind that for a minute!' she said impatiently. 'Tell me, which has more sex appeal? The red lace or the leopard print?' She held up two bras.

'Don't drag me into it,' I said, and threw myself back on to her bed, where her disapproving old teddy bear, Captain, was sitting bolt upright with a face like thunder. I gave him a hug. We would be prudes together. 'I'm warning you, if we don't act fast, Mum and Dad will be dragging us off on the holiday from hell.'

'Don't worry, Mum'll never buy it,' said Tam with a lazy yawn. She wasn't really concentrating. She was smiling a secret smile and staring out of the window. Sunlight slanted in across her head, turning her hair into a halo of gold. She looked like an angel, whereas I was sure I resembled an overweight fiend.

At dinner, Dad waited until Mum had had three mouthfuls of the divine sole with olives, herb and lemon, and then he pounced.

'I've cracked it,' he announced. I noticed he was wearing the shirt Mum had given him last birthday and loads of Ralph Lauren aftershave. 'We *all* go to Newquay!' he announced with panache, beaming at Mum. 'You and I will dine at Fifteen – you know, Jamie's restaurant on the beach – while the girls frolic in the coffee bars or whatever young people do these days.'

Mum put down her knife and fork, looking daggers. 'I am not, repeat NOT, going to Newquay, Jeremy!' she snapped. 'I wouldn't be seen dead in Newquay! It's OFF the agenda!'

Tam tried to look as fierce as Mum, but with

kinder overtones. 'And I've got to go and see Parv that week,' she said firmly. 'Sorry, Dad, I know you're trying to sort things out for Zoe, and it's brilliant of you, but this idea won't work.'

'We could go to somewhere near Newquay,' pleaded Dad. 'A cottage somewhere – near Bodmin Moor. There's all those lovely gardens down there – Lanhydrock . . . The Eden Project . . .'

'Jeremy!' yelled Mum. 'I am NOT going anywhere near Newquay!'

I was watching with baited breath. It was so ironical. There was Dad batting gallantly for England, trying desperately to fix me up with the holiday from hell.

'If you want to be really useful,' Mum went on, 'get online and find us a flat in Florence for a week. Somewhere in the Santo Spirito area would be ideal. Or Snowdonia. Or Paris.'

Dad gave me an apologetic look. He looked quite spaniel-like with disappointment. I pulled a face which attempted to convey graceful thanks for trying, while concealing immense relief that he'd failed.

'Sorry, Zoe,' muttered Dad. 'At least I tried. Maybe you can go to Newquay next year.'

'I'm going to Newquay this year,' I said quietly.

Mum looked up with a sudden laser-like flash of the eyes.

'Zoe!' she snapped. 'You are NOT going to Newquay on your own! You are coming with us even if Tam can't!'

'Tam could easily go to see Parv another week,' I objected. Tam gave me a horrid glare. I was treading on thin ice, but I was determined to make her feel uncomfortable. Why should she duck out of the family hol so easily, leaving me to scream with boredom alone?

'I have to see Parv that week,' she snapped. 'She's going away with her family the week after. I've promised her dad I'll watch his cricket tournament.' Tam had the grace to blush at this series of outrageous lies. 'And I'm worried about Parv. She's never completely got over that glandular fever.'

'Hasn't she?' said Mum with a hypochondriac's pounce. 'What symptoms has she got, then?'

'Oh, tiredness,' said Tam, shrugging. 'Poor old Parv. She needs a bit of TLC.'

'More sole, old boy?' Dad offered me second helpings. That's what he always does when he loses a battle with Mum. Overeat. I declined his kind offer. I had to be lean and mean. I had to come up with a miracle.

And then, suddenly in a flash, I thought of it: the perfect solution to the Newquay dilemma. Biting my lip as I mulled it over, I wondered if it would work out. I finished dinner and went upstairs and lurked on the landing for a few seconds, planning my speech.

Downstairs I could hear one of our *Miss Marple* DVDs. Mum always finds it soothing to watch 1950s murder. I could also hear her talking to Dad occasionally, but I couldn't hear what they were saying. It sounded fairly chilled out, though.

I knocked stealthily on Tam's door. 'Come in!' she called. I slipped inside. She looked up from a huge pile of dresses.

'I'm sorting out some of my old stuff,' she said. 'I'm going to sell the best things on eBay, cos I still owe Dad over two hundred.' For months Tam had been paying Dad back for quietly rescuing her from her money crisis earlier in the year – when she'd spend all her student grant on making her college room look like the Ritz. 'The rest of it can go to the charity shop,' she went on. 'Help me decide!'

Then she looked up and saw my determined expression. 'Are you OK?' she asked.

'Look, Tam,' I said. 'I know this is asking a lot, but if you were prepared to come to Newquay with me and Chloe, it would solve everything – Mum wouldn't freak out if we were with you and we could stay anywhere we wanted. It would only be for a week, and we'd be so, so grateful.'

Tam waved the idea away breezily, shaking her head. 'No way, Zoe!' she drawled, as if it was out of the question. 'Sorry, but you'll have to work this out on your own.'

'But I got you out of your mess when you spent all your money at uni! I've never asked you for a favour in return and I just want to have a nice holiday with my friend. And it would be ten times nicer if you were there, anyway!'

Tam frowned and chewed her lip. 'I'm really sorry, Zoe, and I really wish I could help, but it's impossible. Ed and I have such little time together as it is –'

'Oh, *him* again!' I snarled. Suddenly it hit me. There was only one thing left to do, and it made me feel sick. I hated the thought of doing something so mean to Tam, but I was infuriated by her refusal to even consider helping me out, just because she was so wrapped up in her goddam affair. I took a deep breath.

'OK,' I said, screwing up my nerve in my body and trying not to think too closely about what I was saying, 'fine. Unless you come with us, I'm telling Mum and Dad about Ed.'

CHAPTER 21

Tam's face twisted into hate. 'You can't say that, Zoe!' she hissed. 'You wouldn't do that! That's blackmail!'

'Is it?' I demanded. 'Is it any worse than what you're up to?'

'How can you be so goddam superior, and at the same time be trying to blackmail your own sister?' she gasped. Her eyes were wild.

'What difference would it make to you?' I demanded. 'You'll have had loads of time with Ed all summer.'

'Not loads! Not loads! He can only get away now and then and only for an hour or so!'

'For God's sake!' I snapped. 'Listen to yourself! And think about me for once. I'm working all through this goddam summer, just to make enough

165

money to go to Newquay. No way is Mum going to let me go alone – you know what she's like.'

'It's not my fault if Mum's being harsh about it!'

'Yes it so *is* your fault! You told her about it way before I was ready – even though I'd specifically asked you not to!'

'You know Mum never changes her mind about things like this!'

'Yes she will! If you come with us, she'll be fine about it, because you're supposed to be the *grown-up* one. None of the B&Bs will accept people our age without letters of consent from our parents – if they accept us at all. *You* went to Newquay when you were my age – all I'm asking you to do is give me a bit of support so *I* can go there.'

'I was older than you when I went,' objected Tam. 'And anyway, Newquay's mank. You'll be totally disappointed.'

'Let me find out what it's like for myself!' I argued. 'I might like it! Loads of people at school have gone and they say it was ace!'

Tam got to her feet and stood angrily among the chaos of lingerie on the floor. Her hands were on her hips and she was scowling for England.

'I can't believe you're doing this to me,' she

snarled. 'Some sister you turned out to be! Blackmail!'

'And some sister you turned out to be,' I retorted. 'Grabbing other people's husbands.'

'Oh, stop that goddam preaching!' snapped Tam. 'Get out of my room.'

I went back to my room. I felt like slamming the door but instead I closed it stealthily. I wanted to put on loud angry music but instead I just sat down on my bed, in silence, and listened. Sure enough, a few minutes later I heard Tam come out of her room and go downstairs. I waited, my heart thudding.

After a few minutes I heard more footsteps on the stairs – two sets this time. There was a rap on my door. Even though I was expecting it, I jumped. I'd done nothing much compared to Tam, but I still felt guilty.

'Come in!' I called. The door opened and Mum and Tam came in. Mum had a challenging look. I kind of squirmed, just out of habit. Tam's face looked blank, white and hostile.

'Tam's just had a very generous idea,' said Mum. 'And I hope you realise just how lucky you are to have such a thoughtful sister.'

I arched my eyebrow sarcastically. 'What?' I demanded.

'Tam's offered to go to Newquay with you and Chloe,' said Mum. She shook her head, while looking at me sadly as if I was a baboon. 'I don't want to force you to come away with us. It would be a silly waste of money, and I don't want our holiday being spoilt by your poisonous sulks. I know what you can be like.'

I had to bite my tongue to stop myself exploding at the injustice of all this, but I kept quiet.

'So what do you say?' asked Mum.

'Thanks, Tam,' I said, putting on a bright synthetic smile. I had to try and look something like normal. 'That's brilliant!' I got up off the bed and flung my arms around Tam. 'That's amazing!' I yelled, trying to sound festive.

'Bitch!' growled Tam in my ear. Luckily it was drowned by my enthusiastic celebrations.

'Brilliant, great,' I said. 'I'll ring Chloe now to tell her. She'll be thrilled.'

'Just a moment, Zoe,' said Mum, deadly serious. 'Don't think this gives you a licence to do whatever you want. If I hear about any stupid or irresponsible behaviour, you'll be up to your neck in it!' She gave me a grim glare and then went back downstairs. Tam narrowed her eyes at me for a second, then spun on her heel and stalked off to her room, shutting the door with a venomous click. It was clear she didn't want anything more to do with me this evening – or perhaps ever. I grabbed my mobe and dialled Chloe's number.

'Hi, Zoe.' Chloe sounded a bit dreary. 'What's new?'

'Tam's agreed to come to Newquay with us!' I told her. 'Isn't it fantastic! So we can book into some accommodation and everything will be cool.'

'Brilliant!' yelled Chloe. 'Amazing! Fantastic! Oh, I do love Tam! She's such a star!'

'Enough about Tam,' I warned her. 'You owe this to *me*, buddy, not to *her*.'

'Well, I worship the ground you tread on,' said Chloe excitedly. 'This is the best news this year!'

'Too right!' I agreed. 'Apart from anything else, we got horribly close today to having to go with my mum and dad.'

'Oh God!' gasped Chloe. 'I mean, I love your parents, but . . .'

'Precisely,' I sighed. 'That would have been torment. The history of pilchard fishing and a bonsai nursery, for a start!'

Chloe groaned. 'Let's get some accommodation

sorted, then, shall we?' she asked. 'Have you got a preference? I mean, surf lodge, B&B or a camp site? We could probably qualify as a family with Tam in charge. She's twenty, isn't she?'

'Yeah, in theory . . .'

After I finished talking to Chloe I went out for a stroll in the park. It looked great in the evening light. I needed fresh air, and I was kind of avoiding Tam of course. I felt triumphant because of finally getting Newquay sorted, but a bit queasy because of the way I'd had to do it. I spotted Jess Jordan and Fred under their usual tree. There was even more paper scattered around than usual.

'Hi, guys!' I said. 'How's the comedy coming along?'

'Brilliant!' yelled Jess, her eyes dancing. 'We've got a gig lined up! It's our first, like, proper public gig! It'll be amazing!'

'Wow!' I was stunned. 'Fantastic! When is it? I'll be there, throwing roses from the front row!'

'We're so scared, though,' Jess shuddered. 'I'm going to wet myself! No, I'm going to run away!'

'I'm going to wet myself *and* run away,' said Fred. 'Spraying urine in all directions like a Tour de France cyclist!'

'When is it you're doing this?' I asked. 'I must get tickets.'

'It's the tenth of December at Plunkett,' said Jess. 'It's called Jailhouse Rock. It's a rock concert, really, in aid of Amnesty International. Beast Hawkins is organising it.'

I gasped. 'Beast Hawkins?'

'Yeah – he's a legend, isn't he?' Jess smiled happily. 'Apparently he so impressed his bosses at Major Events that they virtually handed him the gig to organise.' Obviously she was grateful to Beast for giving her and Fred a spot in the performance. I didn't know what to say. I was shocked that Beast's gig was taking place at the Plunkett. I mean, that venue is *immense*.

'The guy makes me feel feeble,' complained Fred, and lay back on the grass. 'He's such an alpha male. Every time I hear the name Beast Hawkins I have to lie down and suck my thumb.'

I didn't really want to diss Beast in front of them, so I just kept my mouth shut. One of the park keepers cycled past, ringing a hand bell – a sign they were about to close the gates. It's such a cute old-fashioned touch – one of the reasons I really love the park.

'Well,' I said. 'Gotta go, I guess. How's Major Events, by the way?'

'Major Events is brilliant!' said Jess. 'We've got a picnic wedding in a wood at the weekend! We're building a kind of Robin Hood-style village with tree houses and everything!'

'The bride's father is loaded,' said Fred. 'The budget is – get this – thirty grand!'

I gasped.

'How's the farm?' asked Jess, as she collected up their pieces of scribbled-on paper.

'Smelly but kind of nice,' I replied with a sigh. Major Events was clearly a very stylish outfit to work for, but who did I really want to spend my summer with – Beast or Oliver? OK, Oliver was kind of slow and shy: if only he had a fraction of Beast's confidence . . . And though I didn't trust Beast's constant stream of slightly naughty grins, I sort of wished Oliver would smile a bit more, or even, well, *at all*. But still it was no contest. If Oliver hadn't been at the farm, though, I would certainly have been horribly jealous of Jess and Fred's summer of continual partying.

As I walked home I brooded a bit about the Beast thing. Wasn't it just like life that gorgeous Oliver seemed so shy, whereas annoying Beast was so pushy! I remembered what he'd said when he asked me out – about how he'd 'always' wanted to. 'It's you I think about all the time. You're the one who's special.' That sort of cliché was so typical of someone like Beast. I knew it was crap – I'd seen the way Beast looked at girls he fancied and he'd never looked at me like that. I expect he was just bored, that evening he turned up at my house and asked me out. Beast probably said that to every girl he tried it on with – he probably said it to three different girls in any given week. With an irritated sigh, I dismissed him from my mind.

CHAPTER 22

By the time I woke up the next day, Mum had left. She had some kind of insurance meeting in Manchester. Tam was still in bed (her job at the Turk's Head doesn't start till ten). So it was just me and Dad at breakfast.

'So, it's all sorted.' He beamed, ladling out the egg-breads with gusto (and ketchup). 'You and Tam go to Newquay, and Mum and I potter off into Wales or Dorset or something. Mum seems keen on a walking holiday for some reason.'

'That's because you are a prize porker!' I grinned.

'Cruel but true,' admitted Dad. 'My study's so small I have to smother myself in Vaseline just to get through the door. Do you want a packed lunch?'

Dad makes five-star sandwiches, so I ordered a

whole lorryload. Our picnic lunches with Brendan and Oliver had become a bit of an institution. While Dad threw cheese and lettuce and salami about, I applied two coats of mascara, and three different pink lipsticks, one on top of the other. I was going to move in on Oliver today and get him to make mad passionate lurve to me – in Latin.

'Cheers, Dad!' I trilled, giving the aged parent a goodbye hug. 'I hope you have a delicious lunch too!'

'Oh, I probably won't do anything more than nibble a lettuce leaf,' said Dad. 'I'm going to spend my lunch hour ransacking the Internet for a bijou love nest in Dorset.'

'Go for it, you romantic old podge!' I grinned.

'Have a good day, old boy!' Dad beamed.

It's always fun when it's just Dad and me, though I wouldn't be completely relaxed until Tam and I were friends again – but when that would happen, with us being in such a turmoil at the mo, I wasn't quite sure.

Over breakfast I'd read my horoscope in Dad's paper. It had said, *'New invitations and exciting possibilities are opening up all around you. Don't dismiss an invitation from an unexpected quarter.'* Maybe today Oliver would make it clear he was mine.

We went into the farm kitchen first, as usual –

175

Martin's usually in there at a quarter to nine, shouting down the phone to all and sundry and giving everybody their orders for the day.

Apart from Martin, who was talking to Prozac and Silkvest, and Sarah, who was reading *The Rough Guide to Provence*, Lily was drifting around in a kimono, making toast.

'Oh, hi,' she said. 'How's it going?'

I introduced Chloe and we stood and watched while Lily buttered her toast and slathered loads of home-made marmalade on.

'God, I so admire you working for Dad,' said Lily. 'It would drive me mad being up in that field for just ten minutes.' She gave us a flirty wink. Sarah gazed at her in adoration, the way mothers do.

'Lily was forced to do weeding from an early age,' she explained. 'One of my biggest mistakes. She now hates vegetation.'

'My aim is to move into a seventeenth-floor apartment in the city,' said Lily. 'And with any luck I will never have to look at another leaf again – except as part of a fabulous side salad, of course. Well, good luck today – I hope it stays dry for you.'

She picked up her toast and a mug of tea and disappeared from the kitchen with a stylish whirl of the kimono and a slight waft of something by Armani.

'She *is* working,' Sarah explained apologetically. 'I don't want you to think she's just lounging around at home. She does help with the farmers' market stall on Saturdays, so she'll be up at dawn then. And she does work four nights a week in a club in town. And she's got a massive vacation reading list from Oxford.'

'She works in a club?' said Chloe. 'Wow!!'

'Not dancing, or anything vulgar like that,' said Sarah quickly. 'She's bar staff. She's got a lovely little uniform: crisp white shirt and pencil skirt. Very classy.'

This was obviously what Lily had told her mum. Personally I had a suspicion that she spent the evenings hanging upside down from a pole wearing nothing but a feather Sellotaped to her bum. But you couldn't tell the parents that, could you?

Martin sent the Polish guys off to do something with tractors, and turned to us. 'Picking and harvesting today, girls!' he said, trying to make it sound like a special treat. 'Brendan will show you what to do. We've got farmers' markets tomorrow and Saturday, so Thursdays and Fridays are always flat out. Off you go!'

So far, disastrously, there had been no glimpse of

Oliver. But as we wriggled back into our wellies and set off across the yard, we heard the sound of the rattly old Land Rover approaching. My tummy did one of its somersaults. But it was only Brendan.

'Hey there!' said Brendan, putting on a primeval farmer's voice. 'Are you lorst? There's no public footpath through 'ere! You're trespassin'! Get orf my land!'

There's something about being at the wheel of a Land Rover that gives a guy sex appeal even if he's very bad at accents.

'Hop in!' He reverted to his normal Irish accent. 'I'll get you started!' He'd certainly got Chloe started. She giggled helplessly as she snuggled down beside him.

'I've got some legendary sandwiches made by my dad,' I informed him as we set off. 'Or will you be too busy for lunch today?'

'God, no!' cried Brendan. 'Life wouldn't be worth living if I couldn't have lunch with you two! And Olly, of course. Besides,' he went on, 'I'm going to take you to my very favourite place today – right down in the valley bottom, where there's kingfishers sometimes.'

Brendan drove us to the field for our morning toil,

gave us a large quantity of big plastic bags and buckets and showed us loads of green stuff to pick for the market stall tomorrow. He drove off, promising to collect us at one o'clock. Chloe watched the departing Land Rover with a wistful look on her face.

'Do you think Brendan likes me?' she sighed.

'Of course he likes you!' I said. 'In twenty years' time you'll be running a herb farm in Ireland together with three kids and a flock of goats!'

Chloe looked pleased but a bit anxious in case this fantasy proved incorrect, and went off to do the spinach and lettuces while I harvested the herbs.

I decided to annex the fantasy for my own purposes and was soon deep in dreams of a future in which Oliver and I ran a herb farm and had three kids called Parsley, Marjoram and Basil, who all spoke Latin on Sundays. Suddenly I remembered my phone was switched off. I turned it on and right away there was a text. It was from Tam.

SORRY I WAS GRUMPY. JUST FOUND BRILLIANT FLAT FOR US IN NEWQUAY ON INTERNET - HAVE BOOKED IT! TAKE A LOOK: WWW.BLUEOCEANFLATS.COM IT'S UTTERLY FABULOUS! CU TONITE LOVE TAM XXX

CHAPTER 23

God! I so needed the Internet right now and instead I was wallowing in dung! I scrambled to my feet and ran down the rows of carrots to where Chloe was on her knees, cutting lettuces and listening to her iPod.

'Chloe!' I yelled. 'Tam has found us a fabulous flat in Newquay!'

Chloe looked startled. I showed her the text and her face lit up.

'Oh God!' she drooled. 'I can't wait to see it! Maybe Brendan would let us have a quick look on his laptop at lunchtime!'

I spent the next three hours cutting herbs in a kind of trance. Mentally I was inhabiting a vast pink palace on a cliff top in Barbados. OK, I realised that the

Newquay apartment wouldn't be like that. I had just gone into vacation overdrive.

'Brendan!' yelled Chloe when the guys turned up at lunchtime. 'Zoe's sister, Tam, has found us a great flat in Newquay! Can we look it up on the Internet?'

'Sure.' Brendan grinned. 'We'll take a look on the farm PC when we get back after lunch. You'll be working at the house this afternoon, anyway, making up the salad packs.'

I joined Oliver in the back of the truck as usual. He smiled. My heart turned over. He didn't say much, though. It was always kind of awkward when we were alone together. Was it because we were paralysed by our hidden passion? Or were we just a couple of boring dorks?

'God, isn't it beautiful!' I gushed, as we drove down to the valley bottom, where the rivulet chuckled along and the sun streamed down in divine dappliness through countless trees. 'It certainly beats working for that hospitality firm.'

'I hate hospitality,' said Oliver. 'Having to dress up like a flunky and hand round drinks to office workers.'

'Yeah,' I agreed, even though personally I have nothing against office workers, because my mum is one, and I can't think of anyone who deserves a party more than her. 'God! It was so hard persuading Chloe, though,' I went on. 'Beast asked her to work for them, and I think she was dazzled by the glamour of it all – and the big bucks.'

'I hate Beast Hawkins,' said Oliver, looking into the far, far distance with a cloudy expression. 'I hate his attitude. Especially to women.'

'God, you're so right!' I agreed fervently. I was so tempted to tell him about Beast coming round and hitting on me. But I thought it was probably more tactful to say nothing.

'He chucked me out of the rugby team,' said Oliver, turning his fab grey eyes suddenly upon me and causing my skeleton to melt with longing.

'No!' I gasped. 'What happened?'

'I should have been vice captain,' said Oliver in a hesitant way. 'I shouldn't really be saying this, so don't tell anybody, yeah?' He didn't want to diss Beast! How chivalrous!

'My lips are sealed!' I assured him, pouting. I hoped he had noticed how nice and pink they were.

'I couldn't stand their attitude to women,' said Oliver. 'And all that bingeing after matches. So gross. So he chucked me out.'

'No!' I breathed. 'How totally unfair!'

'I was a wing,' said Oliver. 'I can run a hundred metres in less than eleven seconds. But they didn't want me there if I was going to spoil all their misogynistic fun.'

'God! That makes me hate him even more!' I said bitterly. I decided to throw caution to the winds. 'He actually asked me out but I told him I wouldn't go out with him if he was the last man left alive.'

Oliver gave me a sudden look. I swam in his grey eyes for a split second – like a brief dip in the Atlantic.

'Nice one,' he said. My heart gave a little leap in celebration. Oliver admired me for rejecting Beast!

'We could form a Beast Hawkins Hate Club,' I quipped.

'Good idea,' said Oliver. 'I'll design the badge.'

At this point the Land Rover stopped and we all got out. The valley was a knockout.

'If you're really lucky,' said Brendan, 'we might see a kingfisher.' We found a great picnic site on the riverbank under some willows and we all unpacked our food.

'Wow!' said Brendan. 'You girls are certainly determined to drag me towards obesity.'

'What do you weigh?' asked Chloe.

'Too much!' laughed Brendan.

'Don't be an idiot!' giggled Chloe. 'There isn't an ounce of flab on you!' And she lurched across and actually grabbed a handful of his tummy! I was amazed at her forwardness, the hussy! I sat demurely on a potato sack, and stared at the river.

Oliver was ignoring Chloe and Brendan. He was sitting with his back against a tree trunk, peering into his packed lunch in that funny kind of way of his. Even though my dad had made my sandwiches, I somehow wished Oliver had made his own. I didn't like to think of his mum preparing little treats for him. When we were married, she'd have to stop all that.

'Let go! Stop it!' laughed Brendan, as he and Chloe started rolling over and over. 'I'm ticklish!' Chloe was tickling him all over – well, almost – while I sat in embarrassed silence eating my sandwich. I wished Chloe and Brendan wouldn't behave like this in front of Oliver and me. It kind of made it obvious that *we* weren't rolling about and tickling each other. Even if Oliver did like me – and it was kind of hard to tell – I didn't think rolling and tickling were in his repertoire. Fun with Oliver would be much more dignified and scientific. We would take tea together in his conservatory and discuss the most stylish forms of bacteria.

Eventually Chloe and Brendan got tired and lay on the grass panting and looking at the sky. I just went on chewing, even though Dad's delicious salami and cheese sandwiches didn't taste quite as wonderful as usual. It was something to do with Oliver. I couldn't fancy him and tuck into my lunch with my usual greed. Love is so tricky.

Brendan rolled on to his hands and knees and grinned sideways at Chloe. 'Never do that again!' he said. 'Or I might have to tie you up and throw you in the stream!'

Chloe giggled madly. 'I didn't realise you were into bondage!' she said cheekily. 'I thought you were just a harmless birdwatcher!'

'Bondage, birdwatching, you name it, I'll give it a go!' said Brendan, crawling over towards the sandwiches. He selected one, and smiled in an enchanted way. 'Never mind bondage,' he said, 'food comes first. These look superb.' And he gave me a secret little grin.

As we ate, Chloe asked Brendan about Ireland, and he told us all about his family, who sounded quite mad and adorable, and his village, the most beautiful little place on a hill overlooking the sea . . .

'Where do you live, Oliver?' I asked, getting a bit fed up with Brendan's boasting.

'Oh, nowhere special,' said Oliver, and he *got up and walked off*.

My heart lurched in panic. What had I said?

CHAPTER 24

I stared in dismay as Oliver disappeared into some bushes. What the hell –?

'Don't worry, Zoe,' Brendan grinned, 'I think he's just going for a pee.'

'Zoe probably didn't realise that Oliver pees like a human being!' whispered Chloe, giggling.

'I know!' said Brendan mischievously. 'He's a god; he pees champagne!'

'Anyway,' said Chloe, turning back and gazing at Brendan with adoration, 'tell us more about Bally-thingummyjig.'

'I'll have to show you it one day,' he said, smiling at Chloe. Wow! This guy was keen! Talking about taking her home and showing her everything! I grinned at Chloe, and I was pleased for her, because although the sight of her and Brendan getting off together was undignified, she deserved some good times.

Soon Oliver emerged from the bushes trying to look as if he'd never peed in his life – as if he'd just disappeared to search for a rare lizard or something. He strolled along the riverbank for a bit, ignoring us and gazing at the landscape. Sarah had told us that this valley was an Area of Outstanding Natural Beauty – well, I couldn't help thinking, so was Oliver.

Eventually he returned to our picnic site, threw himself down on the lucky old grass, and closed his eyes. Five minutes later, Brendan pointed out some bushes a bit further downstream where one might hide and possibly see a kingfisher. It wasn't the same bush where Oliver had peed. I was planning to revisit that secretly, later, and erect a shrine.

'Oh, let's go birdwatching *now*!' cried Chloe, clapping her hands and jumping up and down (she had a lot to learn about birdwatching). I said I was too comfortable where I was. I leant back on the grass and stared at the sky through the willow leaves. My heart was thumping. Would Oliver say anything? I mean, anything special? I stole a tiny look at him. He was still lying on the grass with his eyes closed.

Chloe and Brendan went off and inserted themselves into the goddam bush for five minutes. God knows what went on, because of course they were invisible to me as well as the birds, but when they returned, looking very dishevelled, they reported that they'd not seen a single kingfisher. Presumably because they'd been too busy snogging.

All the time they were in the bush, Oliver kept his eyes closed. I know, because occasionally I took a tiny peep. He was so mysterious! I never had the slightest idea what was going on in his head. It was kind of wonderfully intriguing.

When we got back to the farm, Brendan took us through to the office for a minute and settled me down at the PC. I typed in *www.blueoceanflats.com* and the most wonderful photos appeared: a stunning balcony made of glass and metal with a view down from a cliff-top terrace to a great expanse of coastline.

'Oh my God!' I gasped. 'Can that be it?' The rooms were all to die for, furnished in fabulous plain white and blue and grey. There were two bedrooms: a double and a twin, both en suite and one with a jacuzzi, plus a state-of-the-art kitchen, a widescreen TV and DVD player, Wi-Fi, the works.

'I'm well impressed!' said Brendan, looking over my shoulder. 'What an amazing flat! I think I'm going to have to come to Newquay too, just to visit you and sit on that balcony!'

'You can come, of course –' said Chloe quickly (acting as if she owned the place, even though it was my sister who had found it), 'but be warned: it might not be a tickle-free zone!'

'I'll risk it!' Brendan looked at her with dancing eyes. This was fantastic. Brendan might actually come down to Newquay with us!

'What about you?' I turned to Oliver. 'Are you coming to Newquay too?'

'I don't know.' He shrugged. 'I was going to go with the rugby team, but now . . . I'm not sure. There's a bunch of people going from the upper sixth – I might drop in for a few days.'

All afternoon Chloe and I were in the shed, stuffing plastic bags full of salad leaves and herbs and stacking them in boxes. Prozac was helping us, so we couldn't talk about anything properly (questions such as 'What were you up to in that hedge?', for instance, were an impossibility). Despite not speaking much English, Prozac talked non-stop about the cheapest place to buy designer trainers. He was obsessed with 'karbutzales'. Car boot sales, I realised eventually, not the name of a chic boutique.

At the end of the day, Chloe's mum arrived to pick us up, because Chloe had a dentist's appointment in town. We raved non-stop about the fabulous flat in Newquay, and Fran was impressed. They dropped me off at home, and I ran straight upstairs. Tam's room was empty, so I popped into Dad's study next door.

'Tam came in and went straight out again,' he said. 'She looked very cheery.'

'I bet she was cheery!' I grinned. 'Just look at the flat in Newquay she's found for us!' I barged him off the computer chair and got on the Blue Ocean Flats website.

Dad literally gawped at the photos of the divine apartment with its fantastic glass-and-metal terrace perched high above the sea.

'My God!' he said. 'Are you sure you can afford that?'

'Yeah, yeah, no problem.' I hustled him away from that particular topic. I didn't want Dad spoiling it with doleful adult asides about financial matters – although I did have a slight secret twinge of anxiety about whether we *could* actually afford it – especially since Tam's not exactly famous for her financial skills.

I was drooling over pictures of the marble-floored bathroom when Mum got home. She was forced to admire the wonderful flat, too.

'Trust Tam to go for something upmarket,' she said with a proud sigh. 'She'll have to put in a bit of overtime to pay for this kind of thing. How much is it?'

'Mind your own business!' I blustered. 'You needn't worry! I'm earning too! And so's Chloe! We're all contributing!'

'Of course, darling! I'm very proud of you!' Mum murmured, but she was already on her way into the bathroom for her post-work shower, so she didn't go into tremendous detail about how wonderful I was.

A few hours later, I was watching TV when the phone rang. Mum grabbed it. 'Hello? . . . Hello, darling!' She looked at us with rapture. Dad pressed the mute button on the TV remote. 'It's Tam!' Tam doesn't often ring from the Turk's Head as it's usually mayhem all evening. 'OK, OK, she's here! She wants a word with you, Zoe!' She held out the phone. I grabbed it.

'Hi, Zoe!' Tam sounded jubilant. 'Did you see the flat on the website?'

'Yeah, great, fantastic!' I enthused. 'Brilliant! Well done, you, for finding it.'

'Well, it wasn't me, really, strictly speaking,' said Tam, sounding a bit confidential. 'It was actually Ed who found it, so I hope you're grateful!'

I felt a cold shiver of alarm, and tried to hide my face a bit with my hand – pretending to fiddle with my hair – so Mum and Dad wouldn't spot anything was wrong. 'Great!' I said. 'Of course!'

'Plus,' Tam went on, sounding rather challenging in the way she does when she's really, deep down, a bit guilty about something, 'Ed is actually paying, which is why we can afford it. Generous, huh?'

'Very,' I agreed, trying to appear relaxed and laid-back while all the time my stomach was tying itself in knots.

'And the best part,' Tam dropped her voice to a sensational, melodramatic whisper, 'is that he'll be joining us there. Fantastic, eh?'

Mum and Dad were both gazing at my face as I received this news, and I had the most awful job trying to keep the smile from dropping right off my face.

'OK,' I said, frantically suppressing the impulse to scream in protest. 'Fine.'

'You and Chloe can share the twin bedroom, right?' said Tam hastily. 'And Ed and I can have the master bedroom.'

'Of course,' I said with a ghastly false grin, while my longed-for holiday crashed and burned before my very eyes. What could possibly be worse than having your feckless older sister smooching all over the balcony with her disgusting married secret lover?

'And of course,' Tam went on, with an infuriating, stagey giggle, 'not a *word* about Ed to Mum and Dad. OK?'

CHAPTER 25

'Did you think she sounded a bit drunk?' asked Mum afterwards.

'No,' I said diplomatically. 'Just excited about the holiday.'

'OK, OK, no more about Newquay, please,' said Dad. 'Can we get back to *Miss Marple*?'

On the bus to work next morning, I told Chloe all about Ed coming to join us.

'It'll be OK, Zoe,' she said. 'It'll be fine.'

'How can it be fine?' I groaned in despair. 'All the time he's with us, his wife will think he's somewhere else! He'll have to be lying through his teeth! He might even drag us into it! She might find out somehow and turn up on our doorstep with a gun!'

'Don't be silly, Zoe,' said Chloe. 'People cheat on their wives all the time!'

'Well, I don't want to be part of it!' I snapped, back in Victorian Governess mode. 'It makes me feel scared!'

'Zoe, chill out,' said Chloe gently. She laid her hand on my arm and gazed right into my eyes, and she suddenly looked so fragile and appealing, my heart melted. She'd been badly hurt by that Beast business. She'd been a really good mate to me, always. She'd lent all her savings to me when Tam had got into financial difficulties at college. And now she was trying to rescue our hol from the chaos that Tam had pitched us into. Dear Chloe! She really is the *best* best mate in the world. 'We won't have to spend any time with him,' she went on. 'We can spend all our time on the beach. And maybe Brendan will be there.'

'You bet he'll be there!' I cheered up at this thought. 'I saw the way he was looking at you yesterday!'

Chloe blushed, and squeezed my hand. 'It's so hard to tell what he's thinking,' she sighed.

'What about when you two went off and sat in that bush yesterday?' I enquired. 'I'd assumed the birdwatching thing was just an excuse to get his lips fastened to your face.'

'No, no,' said Chloe thoughtfully. 'He really did seem to be into the birdwatching. Although he did sit right up close to me, I mean, touching and everything, but . . . that was all, really.'

'Well, you weren't really properly alone,' I said. 'Oliver and I were lurking nearby like a couple of disapproving old chaperones. Give him time. He certainly seemed interested in hijacking our trip to Newquay.'

'Yes.' Chloe brightened slightly. 'He did, didn't he? Oh well . . . we'll just have to take it day by day.'

I could see she didn't feel like taking it day by day. I knew she wanted to rip Brendan out of his Land Rover right now and wrap her arms around him for eternity.

The next two-and-a-half weeks *felt* like eternity. First, disastrously, Oliver got the flu and was away for a week. This made the picnic lunches a lot trickier for me. Every day Chloe flirted determinedly with Brendan, and he flirted right back. I started to take a book to work with me, so I had something to read after lunch while they giggled and tickled and he taught her the names of flowers and grasses and stuff.

We did work separately sometimes. They had plenty of time on their own together: tying up bunches of beetroot, going off in the Land Rover to round up cattle that had got into the wrong field, inspecting sheep for maggots. Romantic opportunities galore.

But still Chloe had nothing to report. Well, nothing specific. There was plenty of hugging, because Brendan seemed to be a touchy-feely sort of person, but two weeks on, Chloe was still really in the dark about what he felt.

'What star sign are you?' she asked him one day, while we were out to lunch by the stream. Oliver was back, although he kept coughing in a picturesque way like some Romantic poet.

'Gemini,' said Brendan with a grin. 'A two-faced Jekyll and Hyde, so watch your step, girls!' We laughed, but it wasn't a very nice thing to say. He should have said something like, 'Born under the sign of Pepsi: faithful, loyal and fond of dog-owning redheads.'

He didn't ask us what star signs we were. I suppose guys just aren't interested in that sort of thing, but it seemed a bit rude. Chloe looked disappointed that he hadn't asked her what sign she was. (Aries, actually: headstrong and naive.)

I hoped that she wouldn't be too upset, because if she was, I'd obviously have to spend the afternoon nursing her ego and feeding her toffees. Supportive and fond of sweet things: Taurus, that's me.

'What star sign are you, Oliver?' asked Chloe. This was tactful of her. She knew I couldn't ask, because it would come across as too needy and interested.

Oliver looked as if he couldn't quite remember what star signs were.

'Er – Scorpio, I think,' he said with a shrug.

'Scorpio?' yelled Chloe. 'Wow – charismatic and enigmatic!'

'And asthmatic,' added Oliver. I loved him for being self-deprecating. But I was also struck by how very Scorpio-like Oliver seemed to be. Maybe there is something in this astrology business, despite what my dad always says.

At this point, Brendan jumped to his feet and yelled, 'Paddling practice for Newquay! Shoes and socks off, pronto!'

I refused, but Chloe went for it, and they splashed about in the stream for five minutes, which required a lot of hand-holding and screaming.

'Surf's crap today!' Brendan grinned. It made me long for Newquay so much. The thought of our fabulous luxury flat overlooking the sea was ace, though I was dreading the awkwardness with Ed. If Brendan came, but Oliver didn't, I was going to be a double gooseberry: sitting around nerdily on my own while Brendan tickled Chloe and Ed frolicked with Tam.

By the time we went home that day, Chloe was as starry-eyed as ever. 'Do you think Brendan's really going to come to Newquay with us, Zoe?' she asked. 'He did say, "I wouldn't miss it for the world!" But I can never get him to talk about details.'

I shrugged. I was beginning to feel really anxious, and sorry for Chloe, and guilty about encouraging her to go for Brendan. I was in almost as much suspense about Oliver's holiday plans, but I had kind of managed to cool down a bit while he was away having his flu. I'd told myself sternly that if I expected him *not* to go to Newquay, I wouldn't be disappointed if he didn't, but it would be a fabulous surprise if he did.

The next day was the Saturday farmers' market, and Martin had asked us to help out on the stall with Brendan and Lily, because Prozac and Silkvest were

200

busy with the harvest. It meant an early start: we had to be in the market place by seven thirty. We arrived in the town centre to find Brendan unloading the van and Lily arranging the veg on the stall. She was wearing a T-shirt and jeans and her hair was in a ponytail. The resemblance to Scarlett Johansson was still striking, though.

'Oh, hi!' She smiled. 'Zoe, would you mind tying the sign up to the canopy? Chloe, can you arrange the eggs in the middle, and put a clump of salad packs next to them – and the herbs in their bowls at the front?' We hadn't seen much of Lily at the farm, because she didn't like eating with other people, and she tended to appear, grab a sandwich and retire to her room to be alone with her mobile and her laptop. I'd started to think of her as a bit of a *poseur* and a glamour puss, so I was surprised now to find how practical and energetic she could be.

Soon the market was buzzing with people and a long queue formed at our stall. We were rushed off our feet. 'Hello, gorgeous!' A middle-aged woman grinned at Brendan. 'I'd like my usual two salad packs, six medium eggs and a lorryload of Irish charm and blarney!'

'God, Marilyn!' Brendan replied. 'Have we got

you out of those awful old jeans at last? A mini skirt is it? Well, you've got the legs for it, you could have been a screen goddess in a previous existence.'

Chloe tried to ignore Brendan flirting shamelessly with all his regulars, but her neck went red. It's always a giveaway with Chloe: I knew she was suffering. But it wasn't the customers she was really worried about. Every time Brendan wriggled past Lily he put his hand on her hips or smacked her bottom in a playful way. Lily just totally ignored him, but he was all over her like a rash. Or a puppy. Or a puppy with a rash.

''Scuse me, angel,' he'd say. He even applied his lips to her neck one time, and blew a raspberry. Lily kind of shrugged him off and told him not to be gross. Did she mean it? It was hard to tell. Chloe just looked the other way. I felt really sorry for her.

Around midday the trade slackened off a bit, and Brendan went to get us all a coffee. Most people had bought their veg for the week and gone home. Then Toby and Ferg suddenly waltzed up, carrying a pile of flyers.

'Can you put some of these on the stall?' said Toby. 'Give 'em out to people with their spuds and stuff?'

'What's that, now?' asked Brendan, taking one.

'It's for that new bar in the high street,' said Toby. 'They're having a Brazilian night next weekend.'

'I'll be there all right!' said Brendan. 'I wouldn't miss it for anything in the world.'

'Er – yes you will miss it, actually, Brendan,' said Lily quite snappily. 'Next weekend is the eighteenth. We'll be in Edinburgh by then – remember?'

'Ah, of course, what the hell am I thinking of?' Brendan slapped his own head and grinned in an *I'm charmingly forgetful* kind of way.

'You're going to Edinburgh?' I asked Lily, avoiding looking at Brendan. 'That should be good.'

'Yes, some mates of mine are doing a show at the Fringe . . .' said Lily, sipping her coffee. 'Brendan's driving me up.'

'How long are you staying for?' I asked her.

'Oh, just a couple of weeks. Brendan has to be back by the beginning of September to do another month for Dad, before uni – isn't that right, Bren?'

Brendan nodded. He was eating a raw spinach leaf.

'So you won't be able to join us in Newquay after all?' I asked slyly. Poor Chloe was stacking some boxes in a corner with her back to us. I could almost feel her anguish.

'Ah, when was it you were going again?' Brendan gave me an *I'm charming but disorganised* smile.

'We go on Saturday the twenty-fifth,' I said. 'The Saturday after next.'

'Ah, isn't that just too bad!' said Brendan, giving us a charming but ruthless shrug. 'I'll be in Edinburgh right enough as it turns out. Dammit! Never mind – you'll just have to send me a postcard.'

I knew that at this very moment Chloe's heart was breaking. I could literally almost hear it shatter. But I was distracted by my mobile ringing. It was Tam.

'Hi,' I said. 'Sorry it's a bit noisy. I'm at the farmers' market.'

'Zoe!' Tam, alarmingly, was actually *wailing*. 'Disaster! Ed's dumped me! It's all over!'

CHAPTER 26

After we'd loaded the van up with all the empty crates, and Brendan and Lily had driven off, Chloe and I headed for the Dolphin Cafe. I grabbed her arm and held her close.

'Are you OK?' I whispered.

'Totally fine!' she replied between clenched teeth. She was as pale as death.

'Let's have a hot choc,' I suggested, 'served by our favourite waiter.' I tried to sound cheery even though I was sickened by Brendan's treachery.

It was sunny, and loads of people were sitting out-doors. There wasn't a free table, so we went inside. There were only two seats at a table already occupied by a big bloke I recognised as Dave Cheng, one of Beast's rugby team. He came to Tam's eighteenth birthday party a couple of years ago and I think he's at Durham Uni now. Actually I think Tam had a bit of a thing for him, once.

'Do you mind if we sit here?' I asked. Dave looked up with a dazzling smile. He has lovely teeth.

'Yes, sure, fine,' he said, moving his stuff away from our side of the table. It was a shame we had to share a table, because we obviously couldn't talk about Brendan going to Edinburgh with Lily, or Tam's hysterical phone call, or any of our other dramas. But Chloe looked so jittery, maybe that was a blessing in disguise.

'Haven't we met somewhere?' asked Dave.

'Yes, I'm Tam Morris's sister,' I said. 'I think I saw you at her eighteenth birthday party a couple of years ago – at Luigi's in the high street. And this is Chloe.'

'Hi, Chloe!' Dave beamed. 'Yeah, that was it – Luigi's. How are you? And how's Tam? I haven't seen her in a while.'

'Tam's fine,' I lied. I was certain that, at the very least, Tam would be weeping uncontrollably. For all I knew she was slashing her wrists right now. Although I don't think Tam would ever willingly hurt herself. Her ego's too big. And anyway, red's her least favourite colour.

'Don't you play for that rugby team – uh, the Antelopes?' I asked. Chloe was staring sadly into space, but I hoped Dave wouldn't take it personally.

'Yeah,' he said. 'In the holidays, anyway. At uni I play for the college, of course.'

'I can't wait for the glam world of further education,' I grinned, 'but first we've got to get through sixth form without making total pillocks of ourselves.'

Toby arrived at our table, whipped out his notepad, flicked back the top page and licked his pencil.

'OK, pillocks, what can I get you?' he asked. Chloe stirred slightly in her seat, as if she'd been in a daze, and glanced at the menu.

'A hot choc with cream, please, Tobe,' she said.

'What's wrong, Chloe?' asked Toby. He's brilliant at body language.

'We're just tired,' I said hastily. 'We had a seven-thirty start, working on the farmers' market stall. So we had to get up at six.'

'Horror!' exclaimed Toby. 'How about a massive cake to boost your blood sugar?'

'No, thanks,' I said. 'Just hot chocs.' Toby minced off with our order.

'So you work on a farmers' market stall?' asked

Dave. 'Sounds like fun!'

'We work at the farm as well,' I told him.

'Any cuddly animals to look after?' asked Dave, grinning.

'We work mostly with the vegetables,' I said. 'Not quite as cuddly! Although some of the spring onions have amazing long blond roots. It reminds me of the days when I used to spend hours combing my Barbies' hair.' I tried to look as if those days were at least ten years ago rather than a mere five. 'There's a guy working at the farm who used to play for the Antelopes,' I went on, suddenly realising this was a chance for more info. 'Oliver Wyatt . . . ?'

Dave had been smiley and friendly up till now, but his face fell.

'Oliver,' he sighed. 'What a waste of space that guy is.' I felt shocked and giddy. Even Chloe suddenly focused on Dave, abandoning for a split second her feverish dreams about killing Brendan. 'He just never turned up for training. In fact, he let us down big time by not turning up for a really important game.'

'So Beast sacked him?' I enquired gently.

'Oliver sacked himself,' said Dave. 'He just stopped coming. Beast was very patient, actually. He's so soft-hearted. He couldn't sack a fly.'

'What's he like as captain?' asked Chloe.

'Brilliant. A legend. The best,' said Dave. Chloe and I exchanged a quick glance. 'Have you heard about his rock concert – Jailhouse Rock? In aid of Amnesty?'

'Yes, we know about that.' I nodded. 'Amazing.'

Soon afterwards our drinks arrived, and Dave said he had to go.

'OK, Chloe,' I said quietly, 'how are you feeling? Shall we kill Brendan on Monday?'

Chloe shrugged. 'I couldn't care less,' she said. She seemed to have built a kind of wall around herself. She does this sometimes when she's really, really badly hurt.

'Brendan's a heartless flirt,' I said. 'But he did kind of warn us he was two-faced – that stuff about being a Gemini.'

'I never really expected him to come to Newquay, actually,' said Chloe grimly. I knew she had been hoping he would, though. Hope is such a nuisance, sometimes.

'Nor did I, to be honest,' I said, shaking my head sadly. 'And what about Oliver! I can't believe all that stuff Dave said about Oliver not turning up to training. Oliver told me Beast sacked him because he wouldn't join in all that macho stuff they get up to after a match. He said they were misogynists.'

'What's a misogynist?' asked Chloe absent-mindedly. 'I can't remember.'

'Somebody with no respect for women,' I said grimly, looking round the cafe in case there were any misogynists present that we could spit at. 'A woman-hater, I suppose.'

'Well, I certainly hate men,' growled Chloe, staring into her hot choc. 'They are all basically losers, liars and wasters.'

'There are some nice guys,' I argued. 'What about Toby and Fergus?'

Toby was flouncing in and out of the cafe carrying trays of stuff. He was working so hard, a sweet little moustache of sweat had started to gleam on his upper lip.

'Toby's a girl trapped in a boy's body,' said Chloe. 'And Ferg is a cuddly toy.'

'What about Fred Parsons?'

Chloe thought for a while, shook her head and sighed. 'Fred Parsons is OK,' she said. 'We'll just have to clone him. It's the only hope for the human race.'

I was glad Chloe had managed a feeble joke. It

showed she wasn't totally devastated by Brendan's treachery. But I gave her an extra hug as we said goodbye.

'Hang in there,' I whispered. 'Don't get upset. He's not worth it.'

'Who are you talking about?' she asked wryly, raising her eyebrows. I was proud of her. But I knew she was on a knife edge. I'd have to keep monitoring her by phone and text all weekend.

CHAPTER 27

I had a lot of agendas this weekend. I had to try not to get too distraught about Dave Cheng's revelations. Maybe Oliver was being unfairly treated. Maybe the guys were ganging up on him. Just because Dave Cheng had a dazzling smile and said Beast was 'a legend', that didn't mean it was true.

But as I walked up the front path I knew I'd have to put all thoughts of Oliver on the back burner for a bit: Tam would be in crisis and I had a feeling she'd need my undivided attention and support. Although she'd been dumped by Ed, in a way this was good news, because it would mean that he wouldn't be hanging around in Newquay with us, ruining everything. Now we could just have fun together, the three of us: me and Tam and Chloe.

Mum and Dad were out on the patio. I popped out to say hello and then dashed back indoors. Tam's door was shut and gloomy music was flooding out under the door.

I knocked. There was no answer, but I went in anyway. Tam was lying on her bed, cuddling her old teddy bear. Her eyes were red and black from crying. She looked up feebly.

'Zoe!' she whimpered, and held out her arms. I knelt down beside the bed and gave her a five-star hug. 'He dumped me by text!' she wept. 'And he's changed his mobile number and his email address.'

'Don't think any more about him!' I urged her. 'He's not worth it. Men are rubbish – apart from Dad, obviously.' Tam reached for a tissue and blew her nose noisily. She looked thoughtful, as if my pep talk had sunk in a bit. 'Listen,' I went on. 'We can have loads of fun without him anyway. Newquay will be way nicer with just the three of us.'

Tam went pale and sat up in bed. She grabbed my hand and squeezed it hard. 'Newquay's off, Zoe,' she said in a quavery voice. 'I'm really, really sorry, but Ed has cancelled the flat.'

'No!' I gasped. The room rocked and whirled and my heart almost leapt up past my tonsils and crashed

213

into my teeth. I hadn't realised that cancellation was possible. Our fabulous hol, that we'd been planning for months, going down the plughole? 'He can't have!' I cried in disbelief.

'Oh yes he can!' groaned Tam. 'It was a PS in the text he sent dumping me.'

She passed me the phone on her pillow. The text message was still on the screen. I scrolled down: **PS, SORRY BUT I'VE HAD TO CANCEL THE NEWQUAY FLAT, OBVIOUSLY.**

I felt giddy and sick: I sat down on Tam's bed.

'I'm going to kill him,' I hissed venomously.

'You'll have to find him first,' said Tam. 'I'm really, really sorry, Zoe. I've completely wrecked your holiday with my disastrous choice in men.'

'No!' I snapped. I was determined not to give up. 'We can find somewhere else in Newquay. I'll look on the Internet.' Tam gave a massive, shuddering sigh.

'I don't think I'll be up for it, anyway,' she moaned. 'How can I go on holiday feeling like this?'

'It's the perfect thing to do!' I told her. 'We need cheering up! Chloe's been dumped on, too. Brendan told us today that he's not coming to Newquay, even though he went on and on about how he wouldn't miss it for the world. He's going to Edinburgh with Lily.'

'Harsh,' said Tam. 'Poor Chloe.'

'Yeah, but listen.' I was getting into another pep talk. 'We can cheer her up.'

'How can I cheer anybody up?' groaned Tam in anguish.

'Tam!' I commanded. 'You *have* to come to Newquay with us, because if you don't, Mum and Dad won't let me go! And they'll wonder why you're not going! I'm going to look for a place to stay right now!'

I ran out of Tam's room, threw myself on my bed and got out my laptop. There had to be somewhere to stay in Newquay! I remembered once when Mum and Dad had taken us touring in Scotland, and we'd stayed in a different B&B every night. Mum had phoned on ahead to the Tourist Office and they'd always been able to find a last-minute booking for us. I got the number of the Newquay Tourist Office and called them on my moby.

'Oh, hi,' I said, trying to sound glamorous, rich and about thirty. 'We've decided to come to Newquay for a week, from the twenty-fifth. It's a bit last minute, obviously, but I was hoping you might be able to find somewhere for us.'

'How many of you are there?' asked the tourism woman, sounding, bizarrely, rather Scottish.

'Oh, only three,' I said, as if we would easily fit into a cupboard.

'Are you over eighteen?' she asked.

'I'm twenty,' I lied, stealing Tam's identity. 'And I'll be travelling with my sister and her friend. They're sixteen, and very well behaved. Our dad is a headmaster.' This little detail had burst from my lips in desperation. 'He's terribly strict,' I added.

'Let me make a few calls,' said the woman. 'It's not going to be easy at this time of year. Could you all share a family room?'

'Oh yes, fine,' I assured her, secretly biting my nails. We had to find a room somewhere! If our holiday collapsed in ruins, Mum and Dad would want to know why, and Tam's fling with Ed had to remain a secret. Also, the disappearance of the holiday would push Chloe right over the edge into heartbreak hell.

While I waited for the return call I phoned a few places myself, in desperation. I couldn't just sit still and do nothing. I called some B&Bs at random – I got their numbers off their websites. 'Sorry,' said the first, 'fully booked.' 'No availability till mid-

September,' said the second. 'Sorry, but I don't think there's a bed free anywhere in Newquay,' said the third. I rang a caravan place. Full. I rang two surf lodges. No availability. 'Newquay's heaving,' confided the owner of the second surf lodge. It seemed hopeless. I could feel a massive crying fit gathering behind my nose.

Just as I was deciding to burst into tears, my phone rang. I snatched it like a hawk diving on a mouse.

'I've managed to find you somewhere,' said the Scottish lady. 'It is fairly basic, though. A three-bedded room with a washbasin. No meals, and no en suite.'

'Never mind!' I gabbled excitedly. 'We'll take it!'

I ran back to Tam's room and demanded her Visa card (she agreed but only with a tormented moan), paid over the phone, and then breathed a sigh of relief. Tam's heart was broken, Chloe's heart was broken, the fabulous flat was gone for ever, but we were still going to Newquay, and I was hanging on by the skin of my teeth. I felt amazingly proud of myself for having snatched the holiday back from the abyss of doom, but unfortunately the only person available to admire my heroism was me.

I rang Chloe and told her the whole story, but she

was still so upset about Brendan that the change of accommodation seemed a side issue. I made Tam a cup of hot chocolate and promised her that the hol was going to be fabulous. She shrugged and gave me a weak smile. She knew that she had to come because if she refused, I would be her enemy for life.

We had one more week at the farm to get through before we left for Newquay. It was going to be so stressy. I would have my hands full trying to keep Chloe from murdering Brendan. And then there was the puzzle about Oliver.

I was sure Dave Cheng had got Oliver all wrong, but I'd got a week to do a bit of discreet digging and get Oliver to open up and tell me the truth about the rugby team business. Also I had to find out if he was going to Newquay or not. I assumed, judging by the way Brendan and Ed had behaved, that Oliver would also let us down.

On Monday, on the bus to work, Chloe and I didn't talk much. There was an edgy atmosphere.

'I think we should just treat Brendan completely normally,' I suggested.

Chloe shrugged and struck her lower lip out in a sulk.

'Why wouldn't we?' she snapped. I recognised this

behaviour of hers. She'd grown a kind of cast-iron protective shell. She would never admit, now, that she had ever rated Brendan. I had seen her like this before: after her thing about Beast. She'd been in denial about Beast, and now she was in denial about Brendan. It made everything difficult when she was like this. But it would have been worse if she'd been in tears.

We entered the farm kitchen to find Sarah making tea and Martin on the phone. And he wasn't happy.

'You *what*?' he bellowed. '. . . *Now* you tell me! . . . I've got a harvest to get in – I was counting on you this week! . . . Oh, well, do what you bloomin' well have to, then, I can't be bothered with it all. I've got a farm to run!' He slammed down the phone. Sarah cringed slightly.

'Lazy little devil!' he thundered. 'Total waste of bloomin' space!'

'What?' asked Sarah.

'Oliver blasted Wyatt! Rings me up now to tell me he's just remembered he's got to do a week on a pig farm! This week, mind you! Needs it for his course or something! And we've got a mountain of work to do to get this harvest in before that rain comes in next Friday!'

'What?' Sarah faltered. 'You mean . . . Oliver's not coming any more?'

'No, and good riddance, that's all I can say!' yelled Martin, tossing papers about.

'Oh no. How could he let you down like that?' fretted Sarah. 'And he seemed such a nice boy – sensitive, you know. And charming.'

'Well, I think he's about as charming as a dead dog!' growled Martin. At this point Brendan entered the kitchen. I felt Chloe flinch, but there was no time even for the smallest of small talk.

'Brendan, get that tractor down to the twenty-acre field!' boomed Martin. 'Thanks to Mr Limp-Wristed Wyatt, you're going to be harvesting non-stop from now until Friday evening!' Brendan looked shocked, and disappeared again right away.

Oliver's absence, so disastrous for Martin, turned out to be a godsend for us. Of course, I missed him, but it meant that Brendan was busy with the harvest for the next five days, so he had no time for lunch breaks with us. Sarah took Martin and Brendan a picnic and they had it in the field where they were working. Chloe and I reverted to a sandwich in the kitchen. Most of the time we were alone, which was just fine by us. One day Lily came in and made herself an omelette.

'So, when are you and Brendan heading off for Edinburgh?' I asked.

'Saturday at the crack of dawn,' she said. 'The idea is to drive up overnight, because Brendan reckons the traffic will be light.'

'The crack of dawn!' I smiled, fishing for info. 'Sounds romantic!'

'Well, there's certainly nothing romantic between Brendan and me,' said Lily. 'I wouldn't touch him with a bargepole. He's a bit of an idiot, and he's so up himself it's not true, but he does have some redeeming features, including his own car and a clean driving licence, and he said he's got nothing better to do than drive me up to Edinburgh, so I thought, why not? Go for it!'

Chloe's neck went red with suppressed rage when she heard this. Brendan had 'nothing better to do'? What about our lovely trip to Newquay? He'd promised he would adorn our metal-and-glass balcony, and teach us how to surf. I was going to be very sceptical in future about guys who were all mouth like Brendan. And the jury was out on guys who just chose not to turn up when they were needed, like Oliver.

If Oliver hadn't had any conscience about letting a whole rugby team down . . . if he was suddenly unavailable on the farm at the busiest time of year when they had to get the harvest in, what would the chances have been of him showing up on a date? Maybe I had had a lucky escape.

CHAPTER 28

Eventually that long, last week at the farm crawled to an end. Martin handed us our pay packets, Sarah kissed us on both cheeks, and the Polish guys shook hands with us and gave us their email addresses. Brendan wasn't around, thank goodness: there was no tactless goodbye hug for Chloe to endure. We jumped on the bus home with a huge sigh of relief.

Now suddenly our long-awaited trip to Newquay was right up close. We were leaving *tomorrow* by coach. It was sooner than I'd anticipated, somehow. Once home, I scrambled about frantically looking for my tweezers, my make-up remover, my swimsuit. All the clothes I'd wanted to take needed washing: I had to pack dirty stuff. Our holiday had been glittering glamorously in the distance for ages and ages and

223

now suddenly it had pounced on us and I was just miles from being ready.

Never mind. At least we still had a holiday. Tam had agreed gloomily to come, though she'd been in a miserable mood all week. Mum and Dad had already left for a chic little break somewhere in Dorset, which meant that Tam and I had to organise our own packing, order a taxi to take us to the bus station the next morning, lock the house up, and all that stuff.

I'd imagined arriving in Newquay in dazzling sunshine, but when we eventually rolled into town next day, after a bus journey that seemed to have taken about a hundred years, there was a gloomy haze of fog, rain, mist, wind and sulking. On my right, Tam was sulking about Ed. On my left, Chloe was grieving for Brendan. I was fuming at Tam and Chloe for their horrid stereophonic sulking and grieving.

We were stiff, crumpled and starving, as well as heartbroken, as we climbed off the bus and collected our massive cases. We couldn't face dragging the luggage through the mist and rain, searching in vain for our B&B, so a taxi smelling of horrid disinfectant took us there.

As we drove away from the bus station, signs loomed through the fog: *Pie Mash & Liquor*, *Alcohol-*

Free Zone, Undersea Safari, Surf Militia, Wetsuit Hire £3 hour/£6 day, Pasty Presto, Tattoo Studio. They seemed like messages left over from another era. Newquay was a ghost town, with white buildings fading into the fog, and scurrying figures melting into nothingness. As our taxi climbed up a hill out of the town centre, I tried to fight off a dreadful feeling of disappointment. It was so different to how I'd imagined our arrival. I'd been so full of excitement and enthusiasm, and now this. What an anticlimax.

The B&B was perched at the top of a hill, though the fog blotted everything out, so we couldn't see a thing. The taxi driver swore as he struggled to get our cases out of his stinky car boot, then scowled when we didn't give him a tip. He drove off muttering. We turned to ring the bell of the B&B, a grubby white terraced house with empty drinks cans in the weedy front garden. For a split second I almost wished I'd gone fossil-hunting with my parents on the beaches of Dorset – that's how depressed I was.

Eventually the door was opened by a tall thin man who smelt of cigarette smoke. He was wearing slippers with holes in their toes. I knew Tam was back on the fags as the result of her broken heart and I just knew this guy was going to be a bad influence. He had a face like a haddock wearing a moustache.

'I'm Tamsin Morris,' said Tam. 'We reserved a room for three?'

'Ah,' he said. 'Yes.' He turned round and shuffled off. We followed, tugging and heaving our massive cases up the steps, then up the stairs.

'This is your room,' said our host, throwing open a dirty door. We stared at three beds whose covers had not been washed for centuries.

We were then shown the bathroom (the colour scheme was dead haddock and there were long brown hairs in the bath). There were notices pinned to the wall on grubby cards: *NO BATH'S AFTER 11 PM* (Mum would have hated that so-wrong apostrophe) and *NO MUSIC IN THE BATHROOM* and *ONLY ONE PERSON AT A TIME TO USE BATH.*

'It's all lovely,' said Tam with the ghost of a ghastly, lying smile. 'Lovely. Thank you.'

'Right,' said the landlord, 'if there's anything I can do, don't hesitate to ask.' Then he shuffled off and we shut the door.

'We could ask him to have the house demolished immediately,' I suggested. 'That would be a step in the right direction.'

Tam groaned, threw herself on the bed on the

right, and turned her face to the wall. Chloe sighed, threw herself on the left-hand bed, and turned her face to that wall. I was left with the bed in the middle, with no wall at all to glare at. Bitches! They'd out-manoeuvred me already.

I sat down on the middle bed and started to re-read *Heat* magazine. There was an amusing photo feature on celebs with sweaty patches under their arms and I had already feasted my eyes on some very fine specimens when my mobile chirruped to indicate I'd got a text. It was from Toby.

OUR TENT'S LETTING IN WATER, he reported, **AND THE NEARBY GENTS' LOO HAS OVERFLOWED. I DON'T SUPPOSE THERE'S ANY CHANCE OF US JOINING YOU?**

Obviously the guys couldn't join us here in this hellhole, but the thought of meeting up with them in a steamy cafe was massively appealing.

'Right,' I said briskly, getting up, 'I'm off into town to meet Tobe and Ferg, and if you two aren't up for it, I'm going on my own.'

CHAPTER 29

Two minutes later I left Haddock Hall, accompanied by Chloe. She was still grieving and sulking, but at least she was vertical. Tam had just lain there sighing in a tormented kind of way.

'OK,' I said, trying to sound brisk and optimistic, 'presumably the rest of the town is down there?' Fog was still blotting out everything except the nearest houses. 'Although it would be kind of chic and original if the sea was at the top of the hill.'

I was determined to get her smiling again. I couldn't bear the thought of our precious week of hol being gloomy. There had to be laughs wall-to-wall.

'Look on the bright side,' I said. 'Something really humiliating may have happened to Brendan in Edinburgh.'

Chloe's eyes brightened slightly, and she looked thoughtful. We set off downhill, through a maze of identical terraced houses mostly painted shades of white and grey.

'Maybe he slipped on a haggis and his trousers split up the back,' I suggested. The ghost of a smile flitted across Chloe's face.

'Or a big beefy Scotsman picked a fight with him and broke every bone in his body,' said Chloe venomously.

'Nice one!' I grinned. I wouldn't say Chloe was in a good mood, exactly, but she was at least talking.

The fog seemed thicker than ever. 'God knows how we're going to find our way back to Haddock Hall,' I said.

'Who cares?' Chloe shrugged. 'I never want to go back there as long as I live. This is our chance to pull. The town will be full of fit guys and I'm gonna grab the most gorgeous!'

'Hey, steady on!' I objected. 'Can't we just have a quiet look round together?'

'You can do what you like,' said Chloe in a challenging tone. 'I'm gonna get myself a squeeze!'

I assumed this was some kind of hangover from her thing with Brendan.

'Well, let's start with the guys we know,' I suggested, got out my moby and dialled Tobe's number. When we finally managed to rendezvous with him and Ferg, they were wet through, and smelt faintly of urine.

'It's not our pee we smell of,' explained Toby. 'It's strangers' – though that's worse, in a way.'

'ThereWasAFlood!' gabbled Fergus. 'ItActually EnteredOurTent!'

We'd been planning to go into a cafe for a sit-down meal, but I was worried that we'd be asked to leave when the management got a whiff of the boys. So we headed for the harbour to get some fish and chips. I was hoping Chloe would cheer up now she'd started to fantasise about Brendan being punished for his heartlessness, and I was sure a bag of chips would help. It would have to be just chips, though. Fish is one of the three thousand food items which Chloe doesn't do.

We guzzled our grub in the street. The rain had stopped and the mist seemed to be getting thinner. People were taking off their cagoules.

'How's Tam?' asked Toby, poking a long greasy chip into his mouth.

'Oh, ever since her secret lover dumped her she's

been a total pain,' I said. I had spent hours on the phone to Toby last week, taking him through Tam's heartbreak blow by blow. 'She's spent hours in her room and she's so damn gloomy all the time.'

'Where is she now?' asked Tobe.

'Back at the B&B,' I said, 'having a sleep.'

'We'll have to winkle her out,' said Toby thoughtfully. 'And give her a good time.' He is so sweet. 'Maybe this will be my chance with Tam. I may be a fat boy, but at least I'm not married. Plus I've been trained as a toy boy by Maria at the Dolphin Cafe.'

'Never in a million years would Tam ever look at you, you idiot!' said Chloe suddenly, scrunching up her chip-wrapper and giving Toby a scornful glare. Tobe looked quite shocked. I couldn't believe Chloe had said something so rude and hostile.

'No, no, of course, I know, uh – I was only . . .' stammered Toby.

'Chloe!' I snapped. 'That was a horrible thing to say! Don't be such a moody cow! You may be in a strop but at least do us a favour and keep it to yourself!'

'I am so *not* a moody cow!' hissed Chloe moodily. 'Don't tell me what to do!'

'I'll tell you when I think you're out of order!' I

retorted. 'You're ruining our first evening in Newquay, for God's sake!'

'Well, if you think you'd have more fun without me, be my guest!' seethed Chloe. 'I can certainly find myself more entertaining company than *this*!' And she turned on her heel and stomped off through the crowds.

'Oh God!' sighed Toby. 'I've upset her!'

'No, you haven't, Tobe!' I assured him. 'She's been in an evil mood all week because of the Brendan fiasco! But that's no excuse to be horrible to you!'

'She's right, Tam wouldn't look at me in a million years,' said Toby ruefully, starting to play nervously with the tips of his slicked-up hair.

'Tobe!' I exploded affectionately. 'You're way too good for Tam! And if I could choose a brother-in-law, it'd be you! And Tam adores you, even if she doesn't fancy you – yet! While there's life there's hope, old buddy!'

'I wonder where Chloe's gone?' said Toby, staring down in the road in the direction where she had disappeared.

'Forget Chloe,' I said forcefully. 'Who needs those moods? She'll text us once she's simmered down.' Although I was being reassuring, I was just a tiny bit worried about Chloe. She does crazy stuff sometimes when she's furious.

'There'sALaunderetteSomewhereDownHere,' said Fergus randomly. He and Toby had arrived yesterday, so they'd already spent hours tramping the streets of Newquay. Toby nodded.

'I've got to wash this anorak.' He pulled a face. 'It smells like a zoo!'

'My entire wardrobe stinks like a zoo!' I confessed.

'ButFirst,' said Fergus, 'Let'sShowZoeThe Harbour!'

'OK,' said Tobe. 'The harbour is kind of cool.'

We turned right down a little lane and soon found a nice wall to lean on. We looked down into the mist.

'If it wasn't foggy,' said Toby, 'you'd have the most amazing view of the beach and the harbour from here. Down below.'

Suddenly, as if by magic, the mist thinned. A single sunbeam slanted down through the wisps of vapour, like a golden spear. The outlines of boats became visible on the left: a harbour wall, people walking about. To the right and far below us, an expanse of golden sands shimmered into view, and at the edge of the ocean, a weird rocky island with a house on top, hidden among trees. There was a kind of footbridge linking the island to the mainland.

'God!' I breathed. 'I'd so love to go there!'

'It's an upmarket hotel, dear,' Toby informed me. 'It costs a fortune, apparently. They wouldn't let us in, even if we didn't smell of pee. We'd probably be given the bum's rush by Jeeves.'

Suddenly Fergus threw back his head and began to howl like a dog. It startled me at first. It was embarrassing.

'Ferg!' I hissed. 'Stop it!'

Fergus turned to me, his eyes kind of dancing, and pointed down to the beach. He has amazing eyesight and he'd seen what neither Toby nor I had noticed: a group of guys standing at the edge of the sea, looking at the surf, but not in wetsuits. And in the middle of the group was an unmistakable figure.

'It's Beast!' gasped Toby. My heart gave a sickening lurch.

CHAPTER 30

'Amazing coincidence!' Tobe grinned. And he threw back his head and howled, too.

I saw the moment when Beast heard the howling. He must have got used to it by now: all the boys in school do it whenever he appears. I saw his eyes scan the street and the buildings nearby. I turned away so he wouldn't recognise me. This was a disaster. I hadn't seen Beast since that evening a month ago when he'd turned up on my doorstep and asked me out, and I'd been in a foul temper and told him where to go . . . The last thing in the world I wanted was to see Beast, now.

Hastily I tried to pull myself together. If I met him in the street I'd just nod politely and walk past, but Chloe . . . in her present violent mood, how might she react? Being dumped by Brendan had turned her into a moody cow. Maybe her passion for Beast would revive and she'd start texting him again? We must, at all costs, avoid bumping into Beast and his mates.

'OK,' said Toby when Beast had turned away again and the howling had to stop. 'Come on, let's check out this launderette. Maybe we can attract some fit girls by taking our kit off, like in the advert.'

'I'mGonnaGetRightInsideTheMachine!' Fergus said, grinning. 'MightAsWellSaveMoneyAndGetAShowerAt TheSameTime!'

I really didn't want to hang around launderettes with the guys. I had to keep an eye on Chloe. I had switched into Victorian Governess mode again. I've got to stop feeling responsible for people: it said so in my horoscope. It advised me to spend more time sitting on velvet cushions and eating chocolates.

I decided to go in the direction she'd taken and see if I could find her. She might have simmered down by now and started to feel lonely. I strolled back along the road and came to a games arcade. The noise coming out of it was horrendous. It sounded like one of my dad's beloved war movies.

As I passed, I glanced in. There at the back, was

Chloe – sandwiched between two gross and ghastly boys. One was a tall gothic scarecrow sporting a gigantic red Mohican. The other was weedy with a ponytail and dark glasses, wearing a too-big coat.

Chloe looked up. Our eyes met. Then she abruptly turned her back on me, and headed for a Kill the Fat Zombies game. The boys followed her. Chloe, in a games arcade? This was totally out of character. She was clearly unhinged. I'd tried to be sympathetic and supportive all week, and she'd responded by being horrible to Toby and telling me to get lost. There was no point in going in there and pestering her like some kind of sad minder.

I walked past the games place feeling defeated, but just in case anybody was looking, I put on an expression of deep, excited thought on my face, as if I had a wonderful project cooking. Although, to be honest, I hadn't had a deep or excited thought for weeks.

I tried not to feel annoyed by Chloe's behaviour. If she wanted to hang out with weirdos, that was her business. I gave myself a secret talking-to, and convinced myself I was going to enjoy my hol in Newquay, with Chloe or (as seemed more likely this evening at least) without her. If Chloe remained in a strop with me, maybe Tam would cheer up.

Suddenly it seemed OK to be on my own. It was kind of a relief not to be on the receiving end of a heartbroken sulk for once. I walked and walked and walked, looking out at the fabulous views. Now the fog had gone, I could see for miles – across huge glittering bays to hazy purple headlands. The town had started to feel warm and glamorous, not chilly and scruffy any more. It's amazing what sunshine can do.

I saw a clock adorned with the face of Marilyn Monroe. I passed a pasty shop wafting the most divine smell down the street. Glancing down at the beach, I saw someone had written *I LOVE YOU, SAM* in huge letters in the sand. I wondered who Sam was and felt mildly jealous.

Eventually I found my way back up to Haddock Hall and the elegant apartment which was to be our home for the next few days. As I entered our room, Tam stirred under the bedclothes. I was surprised to see she'd gone properly to bed: got undressed and everything. The curtains were drawn and it was almost dark in there.

'You're missing the sun,' I told her. 'The views are fantastic out there. We had a great fish and chips. Chloe's gone off with two punks. Or goths. Oh, and we saw Beast.'

I so wanted to shake Tam out of her self-pity and get her up on her feet and out on the town. Unless she pulled herself together, it looked as if I was going to have to spend the evening on my own.

'Oooh, Zoe!' groaned Tam. 'I've got such a bad tummy ache!'

Oh no. This was infuriating. Tam was going to pull that tummy-ache act all over again, just like at home, when she wanted to get out of going to Granny's. She wasn't going to come out for the evening with me. She might even be putting on this act so she'd have an excuse to go back home. I'd practically had to drag her here as it was.

'Don't talk to me about your goddam guts,' I snapped. 'Get out of bed and grab your mascara, girl – we're going out on the town tonight, come hell or high water!'

'No, no, Zoe!' Tam moaned. 'I can't! I've got a horrible pain!'

'Oh yeah!' I sneered. 'We know all about your horrible pains.'

'No, this one's real,' insisted Tam. 'God! It's agony!'

'I bet you wouldn't have a tummy ache if we were staying in that glamorous luxury flat with sea views,' I snapped. 'With Ed waiting for you on the balcony with a gin and tonic!'

'Oh, shut up!' wailed Tam. 'How can you be so cruel?'

'Easily!' I told her crisply.

I grabbed my make-up bag and went out to the bathroom. Nobody was about, so I was able to put on my Ancient Goddess of Destruction face. I always overdo the eye make-up if I'm in a strop.

Once I was dangerous and magnificent, I went back into our bedroom. Tam had turned to face the wall again, and the covers were pulled right up around her head. It was pathetic.

I decided to sulk right back. I quickly changed into my least smelly outfit. Green star earrings sparkled in my ears, and in cute black ballerina pumps I'd easily manage the walk up and down the hill.

I grabbed my handbag, checked that my phone and my purse were there, and left. Tam was infuriating sometimes, always trying to escape from situations by staging some melodrama, but the answer was just to ignore her. OK, she wouldn't play ball, and Chloe had disappeared with some weirdos, but I was determined to go out and have fun if it killed me.

CHAPTER 31

On the way down to town I grabbed my trusty moby. I wasn't going to text Chloe: she had to make the first move. Instead I whizzed off a text to Toby proposing an evening strolling around, maybe checking out the beaches and, of course, the beach bars. Tobe and Ferg must be quite fragrant by now.

His reply came back right away. **GUESS WHAT! WE PULLED AT THE LAUNDERETTE! GOING OFF TO A PARTY WITH A COUPLE OF FIT GIRLS! DON'T WAIT UP!**

Although I was pleased for the guys, I was a tad annoyed that they hadn't waited till tomorrow to pull their girls. Maybe I'd have to text Chloe after all. I thought it would be more diplomatic not to mention the row. I could give her hell about that later.

HOW IS YR EVENING SHAPING UP? TAM'S STILL OUT OF IT SO I'M FANCY-FREE. LOVE, Z X.

I walked on down into town, waiting for her reply. The evening was hotting up nicely. Music throbbed from open doorways. There was the smell of pasties and chips in the air, the scream of seagulls overhead (angling for the chips and pasties) and gangs of boys and girls parading up and down wearing every outrageous fashion known to man, and then some.

Everybody was eyeballing each other, and several guys even seemed to be staring at me as they passed, attracted no doubt – or possibly amused – by my moody eyeshadow and grim goddess pout. I ignored them. I tried to look like somebody who was going somewhere intensely cool and wonderful, not a sad loser who couldn't even get her own sister out of bed to keep her company. I kept checking my mobile but there was no message from Chloe. Maybe she'd lost her phone again.

It was one of those gloriously long sunny evenings, and a few clouds hanging above the western horizon were glowing with orange light, reflected on the sea. I suddenly decided it would be great to go down on the beach and just walk about for a bit – get the wind in my hair and the sand in my toes. I walked down over a little grassy hillside where old people were sitting on benches together sharing sandwiches, and a woman who looked a bit like Chloe's mum was exercising her two brown spaniels. It made me feel a bit sad and lonely for some reason.

Down on the beach, though, I began to feel better. It was the same beach where we'd been earlier – the one by the harbour. There were gangs of guys playing some kind of game, and a few little kids who had been allowed to stay up late, still running about with their buckets and spades.

The beach was backed by rocky cliffs, and there was the amazing little island joined to the mainland by a hair-raising suspension bridge, like one of those rope bridges in the Amazon rainforest or something. I walked along, staring across at the island, so I didn't really notice where I was going.

'Hey, Zoe!' came a call. I looked around eagerly. Maybe Tobe and Ferg were down here – having a beach party. Oh no! It was Donut Higgs! Donut is Beast's sidekick, and he's famous for his hideous pimply turnip-like face and gross leering chat-up style. Last I'd heard, he'd been in Africa. Maybe the giraffes had kicked him out.

'Oh, hi, Donut,' I said, sounding massively under-whelmed to see him, and already desperate to escape. 'How was the safari? Did you see any elephants?'

'Man, it wuz elephants wall to wall.' Donut grinned. I noticed he'd lost quite a bit of weight and was deeply tanned. But he still had a mountain to climb in order to register even one star on the International Sex Appeal register. 'Great to see you, Zoe. Didn't know you wuz comin' to Newquay.'

'Oh.' I sighed, trying to sound bored. 'Everybody's here.'

'Where are you stayin'?' leered Donut. He's always trying to corner me and hunt me down. But I was fairly sure he would never find Haddock Hall, and if he did, that Lord Haddock would never let him in.

'Haddon House B&B,' I told him. 'A dive up at the top of the town. We call it Haddock Hall because it smells like rotten fish.'

'Who's *we*?' asked Donut. He's always so nosey. 'Who's the lucky guy?'

'There is no lucky guy,' I informed him crisply. 'It's just me, my sister, Tam, and Chloe.' I had to find a way out of this conversation before he hit on me.

'We're at Emerald Flash Surf Lodge,' said Donut proudly.

'Sounds cool,' I acknowledged, glancing at my watch as a sign I was going somewhere and was already late.

'How's your little mate, then – uh, Chloe?'

'Oh, she's just had her heart broken, so she's gone a bit crazed and weird. But she's not quite so far off the rails as when your mate Beast dumped her.'

Donut looked surprised. 'Beast never dumped her.' He shook his head. 'He never rated her.' He grinned. 'Ironical, ennit? The girl he really fancied wuz . . . Ow!' A beachball sailed down from the sky and hit Donut squarely on the head. He grabbed it, looked around, saw some kids sniggering, and then gave the ball a massive rugby punt that sent it soaring way out into the sea. Then he rubbed his head. 'Few more brain cells gone. Still, it wuzn't my brains you wuz mad about, wuz it? It wuz my five-star body, yeah?' He pulled up his T-shirt to reveal his six-pack with the most disgusting leering grin.

I reeled from this double blow: Donut trying to hit on me again, despite my obvious loathing, and the infuriating hint that Beast had actually been mad about some other girl when he'd swept Chloe off her feet. How typical! Donut's stupid gossip infuriated me. So Beast fancied someone else? Well, what a surprise *that* was!

'Hi, Zoe.' The voice was quiet, in my ear. I turned: it was Beast. He'd arrived without us noticing.

My stomach lurched in panic and I felt suddenly faint. His gang of friends – presumably the rugby club – were all messing about and laughing in the surf, about twenty metres away. I had to get away.

'How's it going?' he asked. I tried to look cool and relaxed, although my heart had started to thud so hard, I was sure he could see the violent pulse in my neck. It was my most embarrassed moment ever.

'I'll go and get that beer,' said Donut, and strolled off. For once I wished he'd stayed. I just couldn't look Beast in the eye. I was blinded by the memory of our last meeting. I didn't care about his entrepreneurial skills, his wretched rock concert for charity, or any of that: I just hated him more than ever.

'Oh, I'm fine,' I said, my heart hammering and my skeleton melting in the awful heat of an endless boiling blush of rage. 'How are you?'

'Great!' said Beast. 'Uhhh, yeah.' He looked out to sea for a moment, frowned slightly, and then turned back to me. 'Uhhh . . . We're having the running-backwards championships. We're going to do a barbecue on the beach later. You're welcome to stay if you like. There's some other girls coming. But the guys are going to do the cooking, and that's a promise.'

'Oh, thanks, but it's OK,' I said hastily. *Other girls coming – of course! His harem, as usual!* Hideous and totally random jealous thoughts scorched through my brain. 'I'm on my way to a party, actually, with Toby and Fergus and some other people,' I told him haughtily.

I half expected Beast to ask me where the party was, and all that, or whether Chloe was going too, or whatever, but he looked past me, grinning at his mates, who were staging another running-backwards race. I watched, too, for a minute. It was hilarious. The guys kept colliding with one another and falling in a heap. But I felt so stressed out, I couldn't even smile.

'Well . . .' He shrugged and gave a kind of awkward grin. 'Uhhh . . . I'd better be going. If you change your mind about our barbecue, just come on down to the beach around ten thirty. We'll be going back into town for a few beers first, then we'll be firing up the old logs around ten. Bring your mates if you like.'

'Hmm, well, I'm not sure I can make it, sorry.'

'OK, cool,' said Beast. 'Well, have a great evening.'

And he turned away. I was a bit surprised. Somehow I'd expected him to go on talking. In the past, whenever I'd met him, he'd gone on and on about one thing or another, and it had been hard to escape, but he seemed different now. I suppose he thought I hated him, because of that devastating put-down I'd dished out when he'd asked me out.

I did hate him, of course. Although he seemed a bit less annoying tonight, and that running-backwards stuff was hilarious, and the thought of their barbecue on the beach was really nice. If only I hadn't had to pretend I was going to the party. But no way was I going to hang around and spend time with Beast Hawkins, especially now he clearly had so little to say to me. Thank goodness.

And anyway, I'd told him I wouldn't go out with him if he was the last man left alive. So I had to keep up the ferocity of my disdain.

I headed for the harbour side of the beach, where there were rocky steps up to the road. Behind me I kept hearing great waves of laughter breaking out. I was so tempted to turn around and have another little look at the running-backwards races, but I was determined to show no interest, in case Beast was watching. Although I had a feeling that, in his present mood, his eyes would so *not* be following me across the beach and into the distance. He had been kind of offhand. If he ever had felt anything special for me, it had clearly evaporated. I sighed – with relief.

As I climbed the steps I noticed a sign: *DANGER FALLING CLIFFS KEEP AWAY*. It made me feel a bit depressed, somehow. A pang of loneliness went through me. It was such a shame I'd had to turn my back on a really fun evening, but I just felt I had to keep my distance from Beast. Even when he was being really kind of polite and normal, like he'd been just now, I always had the feeling that he was, well, dangerous.

And even though Tam enjoyed his company, and Jess and Fred had said he was a legend, and Dave Cheng obviously rated him, Oliver clearly loathed him. Beast was a mystery . . . But so was Oliver. It was all so confusing. I decided I must stop thinking about it. It was making me feel tired, and the stone staircase seemed endless.

'Hey! Zoe!' came a voice from above. I looked up

– and there, on his own, leaning on a railing and looking down at me, was Oliver. *Oliver!* My heart practically flew right out of my mouth like some kind of demented frisbee.

CHAPTER 32

A thousand thoughts raced through my head. So this was what it was all about: all that suffering; the endless bus journey; the grumps of Tam; the temper tantrums of Chloe; the vile fog; the stinky B&B; the inconvenient disappearance of Tobe and Ferg; the awkward reappearance of Beast. All that awful stuff had just been Fate's way of making me suffer so that I would totally deserve this magnificent treat.

Despite the swelling orchestras surging with heroic background music in my head, despite the temporary absence of my heart, which had gone spinning round the entire bay, I had to look nonchalant and cool. Even though my heart and my head had started, in some subtle kind of way, to disagree about

Oliver, my tummy still turned somersaults at the sight of him.

My brain reminded me about all that stuff between him and the rugby team. I realised that everybody behind me on the beach must hate Oliver, and I wondered how he'd felt, looking down on them and being an outsider. Weirdly, it gave him a kind of glamour, though, and I couldn't help responding. I wished he hadn't left the farm in the lurch and made Martin shout about how unreliable he was.

'Oh, hi, Holiver!' I said. I hoped he wouldn't notice I'd called him Holiver. 'How's it going?'

I climbed the remaining stairs which separated us, which meant that instead of gazing up at him from far below, like one of the damned in hell might perhaps gaze at an angel, I managed to reach the same level. Although as I'm about five six and he's about six two, I shall always, in a physical sense, have to look up to him. Oliver looked surprised to see me.

'Oh yeah!' he said. 'You did say you were coming to Newquay, didn't you?' So he'd forgotten. I couldn't help feeling slightly shocked. Had he never listened to anything I'd said?

'I don't remember!' I grinned, valiantly recovering,

and trying to look wacky-but-relaxed, adorable-but-unattainable, blonde-but-somehow-brunette. 'Anyway, here I am! And here you are! Amazing! How were the pigs?'

Oliver shuddered. Perhaps it was my manner, which, God knows, was cheesy enough to make me shudder at myself. Or perhaps the pigs had been slightly less wonderful than expected.

'God!' he said. 'Don't even go there.'

There was a horrid pause, during which I tried and failed to think of a single word in English.

'I was – on my way to the cybercafe . . .' Oliver murmured, gazing at the horizon. 'I just stopped off to look at the sunset.' He had stopped off to look at the sunset! How sensitive was that? Forget rugby. You could wait all your life to meet a guy who would take time off to look at the sunset. And here he was – in front of me.

'Oh, great idea!' I chirruped. 'I should check my emails, too.'

'It's up here,' he said. We turned our backs on the beach and started walking up the narrow lane that led up from the harbour area to the ordinary streets where the shops were.

'How are things at the farm?' asked Oliver.

'OK, though Martin went off on one when he heard you weren't coming any more,' I said. 'He was . . . uh – a bit stressed out about it.'

'Oh God,' sighed Oliver. 'Another reference gone west! Oh, well.' He shrugged.

'Sarah spoke up for you,' I told him. 'She said you were sensitive and charming.'

'Middle-aged women seem to take to me for some reason,' said Oliver. 'It's such a pain.' This was rather a weird thing to say about somebody who had stuck up for you. I couldn't think of an appropriate reply.

'Beast Hawkins is here,' I said. It just popped into my head.

'Thanks for warning me,' said Oliver. 'I suppose the Antelopes are going to be trashing every bar in town.' He sounded rather tired and glum.

'It must be awful for you, not being in the team.' I just kind of experimentally floated this comment, to see his reaction. I was so confused about how and why Oliver had left the Antelopes.

'Well, I didn't have any say in it,' said Oliver. 'If Beast doesn't like you, you're history, man.' I was rather annoyed that he had called me man. I didn't mind when Donut called me man – in fact that was reassuring – but in Oliver it was unforgivable. Had he

254

not realised that I was a girl? I'd once worn three lipsticks simultaneously in his honour, dammit!

It was interesting, however, that he'd stuck to his story about being sacked by Beast.

At this point we reached the cybercafe and entered it. 'Fancy a coffee?' he asked. I nodded. We were going to have a coffee together. This was nearly a date!

'Cheers, thanks, yeah, whatever,' I said, trying to sound like a Jane Austen heroine but somehow failing to achieve elegance.

'How do you like it, white?' asked Oliver.

'Yes, please.'

'Sugar?'

'No thanks.'

Oliver turned to the girl behind the counter. I hated her already. She was looking at him with passionate longing. OK, he'd only been in the joint ten seconds. But it takes less than that for a shameless hussy to fasten her famished eyes on a love god.

Outwardly I was trying to look cool. But inwardly I was kind of praying. I wasn't praying for Oliver to suddenly fall for me, exactly, like I would have been a few weeks ago. I was praying that he would reveal a kind of secret loveliness of character that would put all the disturbing things I'd heard about him into perspective. I was praying that he'd say something like, *I've been a bit of an idiot this summer – it's because my dad lost his job and my mum's been suffering from depression. But they've bounced back now, so I'm going to get my act together.*

I tried to stop my mind from racing through all these scenarios. I tried to just relax and be happy that we were here. Although Oliver was still a mystery to me, he was at least buying me coffee in a cute cafe by the sea. He turned to me. Our eyes met.

'Uhhh . . . sorry, but I've run out of change,' he said with an embarrassed wince. 'You couldn't – errrr, you wouldn't mind paying for them, would you?'

'Of course not!' I grabbed my purse and did the honours, though I felt a bit surprised that somebody as grown-up as Oliver didn't have enough in his wallet for a cup of coffee.

There were some little tables in the front part of the cybercafe. All the PCs were in the back, and they were all being used, so we kind of had to sit down at a table together and wait for one to become available. It was as if we were really out on a date.

As I was trying to cram my massive thighs under the table, my knee hit a table leg and a bit of our coffee slopped into our saucers.

'Oh God!' I gasped. 'Sorry! I'm such a clumsy oaf!' Oliver mopped up the spilled coffee with a paper napkin. I wished he hadn't done it. Though it did give me a chance to admire his long, sensitive fingers.

'So, how were the pigs?' I asked, then suddenly realised I'd asked that already. 'I mean, *really*,' I added, trying for playfulness but achieving only insanity. 'What was the best thing about them? I love pigs.'

'The best thing?' Oliver stirred his coffee thoughtfully. 'I'm not sure . . .'

Another horrible silence opened up, like a gigantic crack across the cafe. Oliver looked moodily out of the window. I was sitting with my back to the door, so I just looked at the wall behind his head. No way was he going to look at me less than I was going to look at him. He wanted to be kind of absent-minded? I would be nonchalant as hell. I even twisted round in my chair. I planned to get my knees out and point them in the direction of north. This would, I was sure, bring him to his senses and remind him how much he secretly adored me. I moved my knees north. They struck the table leg again, spilling more coffee.

'Hey!' he said, as if awakened suddenly by somebody not very pleasant. 'Have you got restless leg syndrome?'

'Ha ha!' I tried for a merry laugh, but it came out as a strangled cry of pain. 'Restless leg syndrome is my main hobby these days.' I had no idea what I was talking about, and nor did he.

There was another silence which lasted five thousand years.

'So how were the pigs – *really*?' I persisted. Oh my God! I'd said it again! I hadn't meant to say it, but it seemed my brain could only repeat things. I stole a glance at Oliver's handsome face. It was, as usual, thoughtful, aristocratic, with very long eyelashes veiling his dark grey eyes.

'To be honest,' he sighed, 'I didn't go to the pig farm. I just told Martin that because I needed some . . . you know, space. I don't think I'm going to be a vet, actually.'

'Oh, really?' I asked. 'Don't you like animals, then?'

'It's not a question of liking animals,' said Oliver, a bit irritably. 'It's just . . . they don't do it for me, you know. I think I might become a pathologist.'

'What's a pathologist?' I didn't like the sound of it.

'Would you have to mess with dead bodies?'

'Yeah, but it's to do with disease, kind of . . . diagnosing it,' said Oliver. 'Laboratory work.' Suddenly he leant back, and did a huge yawn. God, I was boring. Although he was also clearly bored by his future career. 'I might specialise in haematology,' he added. 'I'm quite interested in blood.'

Oh my God! Oliver was a vampire! I'd always thought he looked a bit gothic, and now he was telling me he'd rather mess around with dead bodies and blood than tickle adorable living pigs and treat them when they got their piggy flus and stuff.

'Sorry,' he smiled a thin, synthetic smile, 'I'm shattered. We were up most of the night in a bar.'

WE??? That short word, in all its terrible Bold and Italic, entered my heart like an enormous spear hurled by a very brawny man in supernatural tartan rags. We? We *who*? Who *we*? I could not bear to mention the word 'we'. I would never use it again, even when wanting to visit the lavatory. I would loftily and elegantly ignore it. I would pretend it didn't exist as a word.

Heroically pulling the spear out of my heart, I decided that I, too, would have elegant fatigue. I leant back. I yawned. I stretched. And disastrously, as my mouth was wide open, from nowhere, my throat made a *wurricle*, *wurricle*, *wurricle* sound like rain running down a drainpipe.

'Whoops, sorry,' I said, with a revolting lack of style. 'Excuse me! So – which bars do you recommend?'

At this point my mobile rang. It was Chloe. Normally I would have felt nothing but hatred if Chloe had called while I was on a date with Oliver. But it had become clear that we weren't on a date: we were waiting for a free computer.

'Chloe!' I cried cheerily. 'What's the . . .'

'Come quick! Come quick!' she yelled. 'There's a fight!'

'Where are you?' I demanded, heart lurching in panic.

'I dunno,' she gasped. 'It's got a silver door . . .' and the phone went dead.

'Oh my God!' I gasped. Oliver seemed to cringe slightly. 'Chloe's in trouble! She says there's a fight! In a place with a silver door!' I stood up, panicking desperately and feeling totally helpless.

'A silver door?' He frowned, and shrugged. 'Sounds a bit . . . Harry Potter.' How could he make a joke about it at a time like this? He was so clearly not going to get up, no matter how desperately I yearned for him to help.

'Do you know a place with a silver door?' I asked the girl behind the bar. She shrugged. She was blatantly waiting for me to go, so she could have Oliver to herself. At this point his phone rang. He fumbled with it like a man half asleep.

'Hullo?' he said. 'No, I'll be back soon . . . I'm just going to check my email . . . I'll be back in a minute . . . Just bumped into a friend . . .'

An overwhelming feeling of nausea flooded over me. 'I have to go and rescue Chloe,' I said, helplessly and hopelessly, sounding like a rosy-cheeked heroic nerd in a children's book. Oliver didn't move. He just sat there, kind of shrugging tragically as if none of this was his fault. He clearly wasn't interested in Chloe's dilemma unless she was a microbe on a slab.

'Sorry,' he mumbled, finishing his coffee. 'I'll have to go – Morgan's just woken up. Good luck and stuff . . .'

'See you!' I hissed, and whirled out into the night. Tears burst from my cheeks as I legged it up the road towards the town centre. Oliver was not alone in Newquay! He was with a horrible Morgan! And together they formed a vile and disgusting WE! And all he could offer me in this, my hour of need, was 'good luck and stuff'. And I'd even had to pay for his goddam coffee!

CHAPTER 33

The sun had set, and in the ten minutes I'd been in the cafe with Oliver (or had it been ten years?) somehow Newquay had changed utterly. Now it seemed sinister. Street lights were flickering, fluorescent shop windows glared harshly, traffic snarled past. People shouted obscenities, somebody chucked a burger across the street. I had to find Chloe. Where was the silver door? Who could I ask? And how could I kill Oliver – and his goddam girlfriend – in a way which would somehow cause them maximum pain while elevating me into some kind of criminal-chic style icon?

I ran down the road and the tears ran down my face. I would have to go into one of these bars to ask somebody where the silver door was. Or ask somebody in the street. But everybody in the street looked like an orc or a zombie. And I had to stop crying first. It was crazy. I'd been thrilled the moment I saw Oliver leaning on the railing and looking down at me, and now, only a few minutes later, I was the heartbroken heroine in a horror movie.

I hated him. I hated him for not being the guy I'd thought he was. It wasn't just that he'd got involved with some girl – so what, it was bound to happen. But just sitting there like a plonker and not helping when Chloe so badly needed somebody! This was the last straw. I was so over Oliver, and once I'd rescued Chloe, I was going to celebrate my freedom.

A gang of people loomed up, their shapes black against the street lights. I stepped right off the pavement to avoid them. The last thing I needed now was aggravation. But somebody reached out from the blackness and grabbed my wrist.

'Hey! Zoe! What's wrong?' I squinted through the darkness. It was Beast, surrounded by his rugby team.

'I've just had a call from Chloe!' I gasped. 'She's in trouble! There's a fight!'

'Take it easy, Zoe, no need to cry, chill out,' said Beast. He let go of my wrist and kind of touched my shoulder very briefly. 'We'll sort it for you, no worries. Where is she?'

'Somewhere with a silver door . . . ?' I faltered.

Beast looked round at his mates.

A guy with a big wide jaw and fluffy fair hair said, 'Big Bucko's Surf Shack?'

'Yeah!' said another guy. I recognised Dave Cheng – the guy we'd met back home in the Dolphin Cafe. 'Bucko's has a silver door.'

The gang all turned and began to run along the pavement towards the centre of town. I scuttled along behind them, like a rather fat small dog trying to keep up with a herd of . . . well, Antelopes.

At some point we ducked off the main street and charged down a dark alley. At the bottom of the alley was one hell of a noise, coming from an open door with music and strobe lights spilling out – shouting, swearing, and stuff being thrown about. A chair sailed across the street and crashed into the opposite wall. Beast stopped for a moment and turned back to me.

'Stay here, Zoe,' he said quietly. 'We won't be a minute.'

They disappeared through the open door. I saw the lights flash briefly on their faces as they went in. It was like watching an advert for the SAS or something. I lurked in the alleyway, my heart thudding, biting my nails.

A heap of big blokes came flying out of the silver door. One guy grabbed a broken chair and lifted it above his head – but luckily, he was so drunk he kind of tottered over backwards and ended up lying against the wall and groaning quietly to himself, with the chair perched stylishly on his head.

A couple of minutes later, after a lot of yelling, several figures burst out of the door. They included a small scarecrow-like figure I recognised as Chloe. Dave Cheng was holding on to her arm. I heard the scream of police-car sirens approaching. Chloe stumbled and scrambled up the lane towards me. A police car arrived at the top of the lane, its blue light flashing. We heard the car door slamming just as Chloe reached me. Dave dragged us both into a doorway as several cops thundered past down the alley. Chloe kind of whimpered and held on to me. She smelt boozy and her make-up was blurry and greasy.

'OK?' enquired Dave. Then he peeped out into the lane. 'Good moment for your exit,' he suggested.

I grabbed Chloe's hand and we legged it up the lane together, and then out into the safety of the main street. Well, when I say safety, there was another police car arriving, and the pavements were crowded with people kind of roaring and pushing each other about and being slightly drunk and a bit frisky all over the place. I felt suddenly deeply tired. It seemed about two weeks since we'd arrived by bus, but it was only a few hours ago. This was still only our first evening in Newquay. If life went on at this pace, we'd be in need of intensive care by the day after tomorrow.

'Are you OK, Chloe?' I asked, peering into her face. 'What happened?'

'I was with Leo and Fritz,' she said. I assumed they were the two goths she had been talking to in the games arcade. 'They said there was a tequila and salsa night at Bucko's . . . But some guys at the next table got into an argument . . . Oh God! It was horrible!'

'Have you been drinking tequila?' I demanded, in Governess mode.

'Not much, hardly anything, I'm not a complete idiot!' she protested. I thought we ought to wait for Beast to emerge and thank him for rescuing Chloe, but it seemed more sensible to get home while we could. We could always thank Beast later.

'OK . . . uhhh . . . maybe we should go back,' I said.

'Back where?' said Chloe, looking disoriented and weird.

'Back to the B&B.'

'OK,' she said. 'Where the hell is it?'

I spotted a taxi rank and headed over, arm in arm with Chloe as she was slightly tipsy and a bit clumsy. We bundled into a cab, and luckily as I hadn't been downing tequilas, only a sad little cup of coffee with Oliver, I was able to remember the address of the B&B.

Chloe grabbed my hand and squeezed it, and kind of cuddled up, leaning on my shoulder.

'Sorry I was so horrid earlier,' she whispered. 'I've been so moody recently about Brendan. I was kind of desperate to pull tonight, maybe to sort of prove something to myself. I got talking to Leo and Fritz, and then . . .' She seemed to doze off on my shoulder for a few minutes.

I couldn't help worrying about what had happened to Beast. What if he'd got hurt in the fight? What if the police had got their wires crossed and arrested him? The taxi lurched round a corner and Chloe woke up again.

'Thanks so much for rescuing me, Zoe,' she said.

'It wasn't really me,' I said. 'It was Beast and his mates.'

'Beast?' asked Chloe, looking puzzled. 'Bizarre . . . It was all strobes and lasers . . .' She evidently hadn't recognised him in the darkness of the club. Then she drifted off to sleep again.

We arrived at Haddock Hall and managed to let ourselves in and creep up the stairs without attracting the attention of the owner, the grim Lord Haddock. I sighed with huge relief as I pushed open the door of our room. OK, it was squalid, but at least it was our little refuge for the week.

The room was dark. I switched on the overhead light. There was a groan from Tam. I'd almost forgotten she was there.

'Zoe!' She gave a feeble little cry, almost like a baby. Her normal voice was completely gone. 'Help me!' she croaked. 'I've been sick on your bed, I'm sorry!' I looked at my bed. It was covered with a towel. How disgusting could you get? There was a washbasin in the corner, for God's sake.

For some reason Chloe thought it was hilarious. She started giggling and flopped down on her bed. Tam was kind of sobbing.

'Please, Zoe!' she gasped. 'Help me!' I just stood there, panicking and staring at the horrible mess that was my bed. What could I do? Tam was ill, Chloe was drunk, I had nowhere to sleep: it was a nightmare. Not for the first time, I wished that my parents had come with us after all. I hadn't the faintest idea what to do.

CHAPTER 34

I decided to start by dealing with the soiled sheets. I didn't dare to ask the landlord if he had a washing machine, because I'd have to explain what had happened. I was going to have to use the Stone Age method. I dragged the sheets off my bed and bundled them up, picked up a bottle of shower gel, and crept out to the bathroom. There was nobody about: the place was deserted.

I locked myself in, knelt down by the bath and rinsed the sheets under the tap. It was gross, and I was beginning to feel really annoyed with Tam. Sometimes she is such a baby.

When the worst of the mess had gone, I filled the bath with shower gel and swished the sheets about in the bubbles. At last there was a pleasant smell of citrus. Then I had to rinse them, but I'd used too much shower gel, so it took for ever. I was halfway through the third rinse when I heard a banging sound.

I stopped what I was doing, sat up on my heels and listened. Somebody was banging on the street door. I heard footsteps inside the house and a kind of grumbling. Then the front door was opened and I heard raised voices – Beast's voice! I was sure of it!

I scrambled to my feet, ignoring a sudden attack of pins and needles, and dried my hands. I could hear somebody climbing the stairs and as I emerged from the bathroom I saw Beast going into our room.

'Zoe?' I heard him say. 'Where's Zoe?'

'Here,' I said quietly, right behind him. He turned round and stood aside for me to enter. Chloe and Tam both seemed to be asleep.

'I just wanted to make sure everything was OK,' he whispered. 'I was worried about you.'

'Well, I was worried about you,' I replied. 'I thought you might have been hurt or something.'

'No, I'm fine,' murmured Beast. He glanced over at Chloe, who had started to snore. A tiny smile passed across his face. 'It all looks pretty cosy,' he said. 'I'd better leave you to it.' Then he registered that my bed had no sheets.

'What's this?' he asked.

'Tam was sick on my bed,' I sighed. 'I've been trying to wash the sheets in the bath . . .'

Tam stirred beneath her covers. 'Zoe?' she called. 'Who are you talking to?'

'Beast's here,' I told her. '. . . Tam's had a tummy ache,' I explained. Beast frowned and strode across the room. He bent over the bed, talking quietly to Tam and feeling her tummy. Then he kind of patted her arm and told her she'd be OK – and turned away and got his mobile out.

'Hi there,' he said, 'I need an ambulance. I think there's a girl with acute appendicitis at the Haddon House B&B in Upper Street.' My heart gave the most awful, sickening lurch. I stared at Beast in disbelief. He calmly arranged the details and then finished the call.

'Are you sure?' I whispered. 'God, how awful!'

'It's OK,' he said softly. Then he turned back to Tam. He went over and squatted down beside her bed. 'It's OK, Tam,' he said cheerfully. 'There's an ambulance coming to sort you out. They've got a terrific little hospital here – Wills went there last year when he broke his collarbone.' Tam made a grateful kind of noise and grabbed his hand.

Suddenly I was reminded of the time once when Chloe had sprained her ankle at a rock concert. That was the first time we really got to know Beast a bit. He and his dumb mate Donut had helped her out into the foyer, then driven her to casualty, where we'd waited for ages.

All the time Beast had been holding Chloe's ankle and stroking it, and kind of touching her in a slightly gross way, and it had really bothered me. That was when I'd started to hate him. I knew he had a reputation as a serial love rat and I assumed he was softening her up as one of his victims, and of course Chloe had gone completely mad about him for some time after that.

Now, in this scruffy B&B, I was mesmerised, watching Beast holding Tam's hand, and I suddenly realised that it wasn't a seduction technique, it was the bedside manner of somebody who was going to be a doctor. I knew Beast was going to read medicine at uni. Suddenly it all made sense. All he was doing was giving Tam the care and attention she needed. He seemed really focused and kind of expert. I felt shocked and guilty to discover that poor Tam might have appendicitis, and instead of helping her, earlier,

I'd just shouted at her and stormed out. Beast patted Tam's hand, then started to get up again. Tam whimpered.

'Don't go!' she croaked. 'Stay!' Beast sat down on her bed and took her hand again. His hands looked square and strong. For a split second I felt an astonishing, weird pang of jealousy that he was never going to hold hands with me. At this moment I realised that my feelings for Beast had changed completely: that I now liked him as much as I had hated him before.

My heart soared up my throat and got stuck somewhere behind my eyeballs. The room whirled, and life was suddenly unrecognisably strange. How could I feel this way about Beast? I was in total shock. Thank God Beast was preoccupied with Tam, because I was shaking from head to foot, and I think if he had looked at me at that instant, I would have passed out.

'Don't leave me, Beast!' Tam begged feverishly.

'I won't,' promised Beast. 'Don't worry!'

Quite soon the ambulance arrived and took Tam away. While the paramedics were helping her downstairs, Beast turned to me.

'Zoe – what's your mobile number?' We swapped

phones for a minute, and he entered his number into my system while I entered mine into his. 'I'll text you from the hospital once I know how she is,' said Beast. 'But try and get some sleep. Don't stay awake waiting for my text. You need some rest. Sleep in Tam's bed. Appendicitis isn't catching!' He grinned. I gave a weak little smile. It was so bizarre, falling for somebody in the middle of an emergency like this. My emotions were in absolute turmoil.

'Does anyone ever die of appendicitis?' I asked feebly.

'Never!' said Beast firmly. 'She'll be fine. You'll be joking with her by tomorrow afternoon – you'll see. But you should ring your parents, because they'll want to come down. Don't worry. I'll go to the hospital with Tam and I'll keep you posted.'

Beast went downstairs. I heard his footsteps echoing down the stairs and the front door slam behind him. Suddenly I felt terribly lonely and tired. I could hear other people moving around in the B&B. Footsteps passed our door. Having strangers so close made me feel lonelier than ever. I sat down on Tam's bed and rang Dad's moby. He picked up right away.

'Hello, old boy!' he bellowed, bless him. He

sounded festive. This was awful. 'Everything hunky-dory?'

'Well, yes, but . . .' I didn't want to panic him. 'Tam's been a bit ill, and we think she might have appendicitis, so she's gone off to hospital . . . just as a precaution.'

'My God!' said Dad. 'Is anybody there to help?'

'A friend from school,' I said. 'Beast Hawkins. He was the one who realised Tam was really ill. I think he's going to be doctor or something. He's been brilliant. He's gone with her to the hospital, now.'

My voice sounded a bit trembly. I felt like crying. I expect it was delayed shock. What if Tam died, because she should have gone to hospital earlier? It would be my fault, then. I'd have killed my sister!

'Right, we'll come down,' said Dad. 'We'll go straight to the hospital. It'll take us most of the night to get down there. Are you OK, old boy?'

'Yes,' I said tremulously. I so wanted Dad to be in the room, so I could hug him right now.

'Good girl!' said Dad. 'Try to get some sleep – we'll be there first thing tomorrow morning. I'm sure she'll be OK.' And then he was gone.

I stretched out on Tam's bed, feeling utterly limp and weak. The pillow smelt of her moisturiser. I stared idly at my mobile, scrolling through the memory. Beast's number was in there. *Harry Hawkins*, it said. Harry! So that was Beast's real name! It suited him, somehow. I was glad he'd put 'Harry' not 'Beast'. I was trying to figure out why, exactly, when my moby started to ring. It made me jump for a minute, but then I got a grip. I had to. This would be Mum having her hysterics. I took a deep breath.

CHAPTER 35

After I'd told Mum everything I'd just told Dad, all over again, and tried to get her to calm down, eventually she rang off. 'We're driving down through the night!' she said dramatically. 'We'll see you tomorrow, darling. Let us know if there's any change.'

'Yeah, yeah,' I assured her.

Once she'd rung off, I relaxed slightly. Chloe was snoring gently. The street seemed quiet. Then I heard footsteps on the stairs. They came closer: along the landing. There was a knock on our door. I leapt up and went to answer it. Suddenly I was horribly aware that there wasn't a chain on it or anything. Never mind. If it was the axe-man, I'd just have to kick him in the masculine department. I opened the door a crack and peeped out. It was Lord Haddock himself, complete with the smell of stale cigarette smoke and the dismal moustache.

'What's going on?' he demanded. 'Why are there sheets in the bath?' I remembered, with a sickening jolt, my earlier attempts at laundering.

'Sorry, sorry,' I said. 'My sister's been taken to hospital. We think she's got appendicitis.' He looked suspicious. 'She was sick.' He pulled a disgusted face.

'Charming!' he sneered.

'I was only trying to wash them,' I explained.

'Typical! You young people,' he grumbled. 'You're a law unto yourselves. And while I'm on the subject, we have a strict No Visitors rule,' he went on. 'And your friend who made such a racket hammering on the door pushed past me as if he owned the place!'

'I'm sorry,' I said. 'But it was an emergency.'

'So who else is in there with you now?' he demanded.

'Nobody!' I snapped. I could do without this hassle. I opened the door wide and invited him to inspect the room, but I was really pissed off at his suspicious attitude and let him know it with a fearful scowl and sneer. He took a quick look. The tableau included Chloe snoring. It was the picture of innocence.

'I'm not very happy about this,' whinged the landlord.

'I'm not very happy about it!' I snapped. Poor Tam was dangerously ill and we needed support and understanding, not hassle. 'My sister's seriously ill and she could have died! And I'm trying to wash your goddam sheets! What more do you want?'

'Don't you take that tone with me!' said Lord Haddock, in a quiet and deadly voice.

'I'm not taking an attitude!' I shouted. 'My sister's just been taken to hospital!'

'Please keep your voice down,' he murmured menacingly. 'You're disturbing the other guests. I can't have this. I'm going to have to ask you to leave in the morning. I want you out by ten. I'm not having under-eighteens in here unsupervised. It always leads to trouble.'

And he turned on his heel and marched off, muttering, 'Blasted kids', before I could tell him it would be a pleasure to vacate this hellhole and I hoped his next guests would poo on the ceiling. I decided not to text Mum and Dad about us being chucked out of the B&B. They had enough to worry about already.

I didn't sleep very well, with tortured dreams about Beast and Tam. Chloe was snoring and slurping in her sleep and muttering things. I kept jolting awake. Then, around 3 a.m., I'd just fallen into another of my light, tormented dozes when my phone buzzed. It was a text from somebody called Harry Hawkins. *Who the . . .?* I frowned for a moment, but then realised it was, of course, Beast.

HEY ZOE. TAM'S OK - THOUGH MINUS HER APPENDIX. SLEEP WELL.

I heaved a huge sigh of relief. It seemed poor old Tam was going to live. I was so relieved, I had a little cry.

At the crack of dawn (or eight thirty to be honest) I was awoken again by my phone buzzing. I grabbed it.

'Zoe!' It was Mum. 'We're at the hospital! Tam's fine! She's had her appendix out and she's a bit groggy but she's on the road to recovery.'

'I know, yeah, thank goodness,' I said. 'Beast sent me a text.'

'The surgeon says it was just in time,' said Mum. 'If it had been left any longer it could have been critical.'

'God!' I gasped. 'Horrible!'

'We're going to have some breakfast,' said Mum, 'and then we'll come round to your B&B. I don't suppose they've got a spare room available, have they? Dad and I are going to need somewhere.'

I informed Mum that the only room likely to be available was ours, as we were being thrown out and had to vacate by ten o'clock. I also confided a few choice details about the accommodation, which made her realise that she would rather sleep in a ditch than between Lord Haddock's grim, grey, horror-film sheets.

'How ghastly!' said Mum. 'Don't worry. We'll find somewhere nice. You can move in with us.'

'And Chloe,' I reminded her.

'And Chloe, of course,' confirmed Mum, giving a martyred sigh. She has this act which suggests that Chloe's mum is totally irresponsible, and if Chloe ever manages to grow up into a civilised adult, it will be my mum's proud achievement, not Chloe's mum's. 'We'll find somewhere,' she said in steely mode. 'But it might be out of town.'

I felt so tired, I wouldn't have cared if the accommodation was in Argentina. Mum rang off, hell-bent on locating croissants and a B&B with sanded wood floors, chic china washbasins and thick, heavy cotton sheets that smelt of lavender.

At this moment Chloe woke up. 'Zoe!' she croaked. 'Did Tam get taken off in an ambulance last night, or did I dream it?' Before I could fill her in on the ghastly details of the last few hours, my moby buzzed again. It was a text from Tobe.

SPENT LAST NIGHT ON THE STATION PLATFORM, it said. **AVOIDING WEREWOLVES. DITCHED BY GIRLS WHEN THEY MET HANDSOMER AND RICHER GUYS. MET OLIVER WYATT IN TOWN WITH TERRIBLE GIRL CALLED MORGAN. WHAT'S THE NEWS FROM ZOELAND?**

OH NOTHING MUCH, I replied. **TAM IN HOSPITAL, AND WE'VE BEEN CHUCKED OUT OF OUR B&B. BEAT THAT!** Though shattered to find that Oliver had indeed brought a female companion, I was intrigued to hear that she was 'terrible', and I was kind of looking forward to inspecting her as soon as possible.

CHAPTER 36

'I hate all men,' announced Chloe as we packed our bags. 'I knew Lord Haddock would turn out to be a total pig, just like Brendan and those horrible guys I got trapped with last night.'

'What was the fight about?' I asked.

'Oh, nothing,' sighed Chloe. 'You know. Caveman stuff. All that testosterone.'

'Beast did rescue us last night, though,' I said. 'It was great having a kind of army of guys on our side. And he was really, really sensible and focused. He was the only person who realised how ill Tam was. And he organised getting her to hospital and everything.' Chloe stopped packing for a minute and frowned.

'Was I asleep?' she asked. 'Did he see me asleep? Did I have my mouth open?'

'No, no,' I assured her. 'We were totally concentrating on Tam, and you were right under the bedclothes, anyway, and . . .'

'Not that I care,' Chloe went on. 'I'm not going to waste any time on men any more, and anyway, Beast is history.' I couldn't think of anything to say. 'I'm going to give myself a makeover,' said Chloe. 'I'm going to become the Iron Maiden. I might even get a tattoo.'

If Chloe was going to redesign herself, I might just have to join in. I felt deeply dissatisfied with myself. I was so unfit, for a start. I began to plan a programme of running. I wondered how long it would take me to look good in Lycra shorts. Right now, I would look like an airbag.

We left the B&B in a taxi, and went to the hospital with all our luggage. There was nowhere else to go: we were homeless. We arrived at the hospital and found our way to Tam's bedside, where Dad was sitting doing a crossword in a relaxed way.

I peeped at Tam. She seemed to be dozing. Her face was pale and there were several horrid tubes coming out from under the bedclothes. Dad gave me a big hug, and then hugged Chloe as well, just to be polite.

'Mum's gone off to look for a place to stay,' he

whispered. 'Tam's asleep most of the time. She's going to be fine.'

'What are those tubes?' I asked.

'Oh, just one to take the blood away, and one to take the pee away, and a drip line into the back of her hand to give her bacon and eggs straight into the vein – that sort of thing,' mused Dad. 'I expect there's one supplying Calvin Klein as well.'

I was so glad it was Dad on guard at Tam's bedside. His jokes made everything just slightly less tragic and gross. Mum's so tense, she would have increased the stress levels by cleaning the floor with wet tissues, or something.

I stared at Tam. Her beautiful face was so white and there were shadows under her eyes. Her lips were a bit cracked and dry. There was a bruise on her hand where the drip went in. You could tell she'd been through something really awful. As I looked at her my heart kind of squeezed with anguish for a split second. My lovely sister was so fragile.

I didn't care any more that she was so much more beautiful than me. I didn't care that she could be irritating, that she manipulated Mum, that she behaved irresponsibly, that she was hopeless with money and reckless in love. I just wanted her to get better and never be ill again for the rest of her life. I'd happily take on her share of illnesses in future, and I made a mental note to God to arrange this, if possible.

'So what are your plans for the holiday, Chloe?' asked Dad, putting his crossword away politely even though I knew he would much rather finish it.

'I've got plenty of plans,' said Chloe firmly. 'But they most definitely do not include meeting boys.'

'Oh, right,' said Dad. 'Reassuring, I suppose. So what are these plans, then?'

'Well, for a start, I'm going to the girls-only surf school,' said Chloe. I was startled. I didn't know anything about this. Presumably it was something Chloe had heard about last night, behind the silver door, before the fight had broken out. I would have to make it crystal clear that when it came to big waves, I'd be watching from the beach. 'I'm going to look into fitness and yoga too,' she went on. 'I'd like to do yoga on the beach; I think that'd be really cool. Plus I'm thinking about getting a tattoo.'

Dad blinked slightly and raised his eyebrows a tad, but he didn't comment. He was being tactful for once.

'Only a henna tattoo,' I added. 'It'll fade away in a few weeks.'

'No, Zoe! A proper tattoo!' said Chloe fiercely. I shrugged. Chloe's mum has a tattoo, actually. She's got the god Mercury on her left shoulder.

'And what are your plans, old boy?' asked Dad. I scratched my head.

'I want to meet this girl called Morgan,' I said. 'Oliver Wyatt – he's a guy from school and he was working on the farm with us – he's got a girlfriend and apparently she's awful.'

'One can see how that might be an enjoyable project,' said Dad. 'But I'm not sure it's realistic to build an entire holiday around it.'

Poor Dad! How little he knew!

After a while Mum reappeared, looking very tired but wearing plenty of lipstick as usual. She wears a special purplish-pink one in emergencies. She made such a fuss of me and Chloe that Tam woke up. Then Mum made a fuss of Tam, which seemed to set back Tam's recovery for about a fortnight.

Eventually a nurse tactfully suggested that we should push off and take our suffocating love elsewhere.

'I've found a flat,' said Mum as we crossed the hospital car park. 'There was a last-minute cancellation, apparently. We've been very lucky.'

She drove us across town, down through some snaky lanes and up another hillside, then out on to a cliff top with amazing views. She parked and we all got out.

'Come on!' said Mum with a grin, waving the keys. 'It may be a bit extravagant, but I think we all need a little treat.'

There was an apartment building on the right, glistening white in the sun, with stylish blue window frames and shutters, a bit like a house in Greece or something. And there was a sign: *BLUE OCEAN FLATS*.

My heart missed a beat. These were the flats where Tam had been going to take us with her married man! I tried to catch Chloe's eye, but she was staring at the amazing views and didn't seem to have noticed.

Mum led us friskily to the main door and on through into apartment No. 2. We entered and gasped. It was *exactly* the same one we would have stayed in! It was all there – the amazing cantilevered balcony, all metal and glass, with the stupendous view of the vast beach, where tiny people were running about like ants hundreds of feet below.

'Nice kitchen,' said Mum approvingly, stroking the

granite worktops. She adores granite – sometimes I think she wishes Dad was made out of it. Dad had plonked himself down on the sofa. Thank God they didn't seem to recognise the apartment as the one we'd originally been planning to stay in – after all, they'd only seen the briefest glimpse of the website, weeks ago.

'Oh my God!' gasped Chloe suddenly, 'this is the apartment we were going to stay in with Tam, with Ed, before it all went wrong . . .'

Trust Chloe! I tried to shush her, but it was too late. In a split second Chloe realised she shouldn't have opened her big mouth, and clapped her hand across it, looking guilty. Mum looked up sharply. Even Dad seemed mildly interested.

'Who's this Ed?' pounced Mum. 'And how did it all go wrong? And how in the world were you ever going to afford this place? I can hardly afford it myself!'

CHAPTER 37

'Oh, he was just some guy Tam was mixed up with,' I said, trying to make it all sound terribly unimportant. 'It's over now. He dumped her.'

'Who was he?' Mum looked shocked. How could any man on earth dump her baby, especially a man who could afford a week in this palace?

'Oh, some guy . . .' I shrugged and strolled towards the balcony as fast as my little legs would carry me. 'A businessman.'

'How old was he?' demanded Mum. I shrugged again. Any minute now I would sprain my shrugging muscles. 'And why did Chloe look so guilty for even mentioning him?' She turned on Chloe, who literally cringed. She was still covering her mouth with her hand, like somebody in a comic.

My mind raced. I could so *not* tell Mum Ed was a married man. She would never give Tam any peace. I had to think of something.

'Tam didn't want you to know about him,' I said, trying to sound casual. What could I say? There had to be something about Ed which Mum would despise. Despising is her favourite emotion. Hundreds of images flickered through my mind: glimpses of men, or types of men, my mum has despised over the years. It was quite an archive.

The Prime Minister, paedophiles, arms dealers, mass murderers, scroungers and spongers, people who eat imported strawberries in January, show-offs who drive Porsches too fast through suburbs . . . men with pony tails . . .

'It was just that Ed was a mass murderer, Mum. I mean, he was a lovely guy and everything, but there were five bodies under his patio.' . . . 'Well, it wouldn't have mattered, as long as Tam was happy.' . . . 'But Mum, he eats strawberries in January!' . . . 'The irresponsible idiot! How could she ever get involved with anyone like that? I'm going to lock her in a tower till she's thirty!'

'He was . . .' It had to be dull, too. I didn't want Mum looking him up on the Internet. He couldn't be an artist who made sculptures out of elephant dung.

(Though I hear they're becoming very commercial.) Suddenly I thought of it: 'He smokes!'

Mum's eyes narrowed in hatred.

'And drinks! – Like, for England!'

'I wonder what on earth she ever saw in him, then,' snapped Mum, losing interest nicely and sliding into comfy contempt (one of her other fave emotions). 'How did he make his money?' she demanded, hands on hips, her eyes swivelling all around our luxury apartment. 'If he was going to pay for all this?'

I shrugged again.

'The Internet,' I said. Thank God for the web! However did the cavemen manage, back in the 1950s?

'Oh, look! There's a pair of binoculars,' said Dad, suddenly leaping up and heading for a shelf. Dear old Dad. Trust him to change the subject from things uncomfortably near home to things far away – so far away, you need binoculars.

We all went out on to the balcony and scanned the beach in turn. I was hoping for a glimpse of Oliver on the arm of a fat tyrant but I couldn't see anybody who even looked like anybody I knew.

My phone bleeped. It was a message from Beast.

WHERE ARE YOU? I WENT BACK TO B&B AND SATAN SAID YOU'D LEFT. My heart started to race. A wave of totally new, thrilling excitement swept through me. He had called at the B&B, hoping to see us! How soon could I get him here? I knew Mum and Dad would want to thank him for helping last night, so I had the perfect excuse to invite him.

Hastily, with trembling fingers, I composed a reply. **MY PARENTS HAVE RENTED AMAZING APARTMENT No. 2 BLUE OCEAN FLATS. GREAT VIEW. JUST PAST THE BIG GREEN CINEMA. COME UP AND SEE US! (NOW IF POSS?)**

An answer whizzed back right away. **GOT A BEACH RUGBY MATCH THIS MORNING — MAYBE CATCH YOU LATER.** I felt my stomach sink with disappointment. This was so, so weird. Just yesterday I was hoping to avoid bumping into Beast, now I'd kill to get a glimpse of him across a crowded room.

When I told Chloe there was a beach rugby match scheduled, her eyes lit up. 'Let's go!' She grinned. 'I love to watch guys beating one another into a pulp!'

I was relieved that she wanted to go down and watch the match. It was good to see her cheerful and full of beans again after so much heartbroken sulking. But I was going to have to keep quiet about my feelings for Beast, for a while at least – until I'd got used to them, if nothing else.

We checked our make-up, fired off a text to Toby and Fergus to meet us on the beach, and headed out. The parents stayed behind, planning to doze and chill out after their long drive through the night.

The beach was awesome: a huge bowl of brilliant light, towering cliffs on all sides, and surfers riding the waves and toppling in with graceful crashes. It wasn't the rocky little beach by the harbour where I had met Beast on the previous day. It was a vast airy space of thundering waves and rainbow spray and ripping wind which thrashed against our bodies, making us scream in delight. Toby and Fergus appeared in the distance – a dot and a little dot. Toby rang me on my moby. 'I'm on the beach!' he yelled.

'I can see you, you moron!' I yelled back. We met with much hugging and I was glad to find the boys no longer smelt of urine. One's always grateful for those little courtesies.

'Ferg and I are going to learn to surf, but not till tomorrow!' shouted Tobe, as the wind ruffled all the little golden tips of his sticking-up hair. 'First I have to learn to embroider cushions and make strawberry jam!'

'WeJustSawBeastAndHisTeam,' said Ferg. 'The Antelopes!'

'The game starts in five!' said Toby. 'Come on, let's get back there!'

My heart started racing in a mad, giddy way. In just a couple of minutes I was going to see Beast again. I tried to control my emotions, but it was impossible. I had fallen for him with a truly deafening crash, but it was all so painful: I knew that I was the one girl on earth he would never, ever ask out. If only I could go back in time, I would act so very differently. But what could I do? Short of starting all over again, what hope was there? We set out, walking into the wild wind, towards the crowds of guys about three hundred metres away. I couldn't see which was Beast, but I knew he was there. I had to find a way of starting over again. There had to be a way.

'Hey, Zoe!' I turned, and with a strange, jarring jolt I saw Oliver, with a girl wrapped round him, her dark hair streaming in the wind. 'Morgan,' said Oliver. 'This is Zoe and Chloe and Toby and Fergus. Guys, this is Morgan.'

Morgan wasn't exactly the girlfriend I would have selected for Oliver. I would have chosen a lardass or Miss Potato Head or somebody with an extensive handlebar moustache. Morgan was petite and her dark shiny hair was snaking about in the wind, and her eyes were huge and melting like a puppy's.

'Hi, guys!' Morgan smiled, fastening herself even more closely to Oliver's torso. She was as completely wrapped round him as a tortilla around some refried beans. Oliver looked slightly uneasy, and, to be honest, cheesy. This was wonderful. I had fallen out of love with him just in the nick of time.

'Oh, hi, Morgan! Are you going to watch the rugby?' asked Chloe.

'No way!' said Morgan decisively. 'They kicked Olly out of the team because he didn't want to join in their moronic lifestyle. Beast dumped him. He's such a prat.' A soaring rocket of indignation suddenly shot through my insides. How dare she diss the adorable Beast?

'Oh, really?' I said icily. 'I heard Oliver had dropped out himself because he couldn't be bothered to turn up for training.' Oliver flinched and blushed. 'And didn't even turn up for some of the matches,' I added.

Morgan frowned and looked up at her beau. He managed to squeeze out a tiny ironical smile from somewhere.

'There may be a grain of truth in that.' He shrugged. 'But what those guys don't realise is, there's more to life than rugby.'

'They'll be starting in a min,' said Chloe, looking down the beach to where the teams were gathering.

'Come on, Olly!' commanded Morgan. 'We're going shopping.' Oliver looked embarrassed at the word *shopping*. He clearly didn't want us to think he was a big girl's blouse. He and Morgan strolled off, and our little gang turned our faces to the wild wind again. Toby slid in beside me and gripped my arm.

'Hang in there, Zoe, pet!' he whispered. 'I heard them having a row earlier. He'll soon get tired of her, and he'll realise how goddam perfect you are!'

'No thanks, Toby!' I shook my head. 'I am so over that guy.'

'Wow!' said Fergus. 'SomeFitGirlThough!'

'Mmmm,' agreed Toby. 'Ten out of ten for sex appeal.' The swine! He was supposed to say, 'Oh, no, Ferg, she's all cheap tricks, she can't compete with Zoe!' Toby still has a lot to learn.

The rugby had started when we arrived. It was brilliant, watching it with a backdrop of shining surf. We witnessed several bone-crunching tackles and saw the flying spit and heard the manly grunts.

I realised, with a thrill, that Beast was an ace per-
former. He could run really fast and he was muscular
and strong. He scored two tries and at the end of the
match he was lifted up shoulder high by his team,
who carried him to the water's edge and chucked him
in the sea. I think it was some kind of sacrifice to the
gods.

After the match, Beast and his mates seemed to be
heading somewhere important: a shower block, presumably, because by now all of them were dripping
with sea-water and lightly dusted with sodden sand.

'It's like a wet T-shirt competition,' whispered
Toby. 'It's almost enough to turn me gay!'

I'd half expected Beast to come over and talk to us,
but he gave us a cheery wave and was clearly too busy
with his mates. I felt a stupid disappointment that he
was going away, even if it was only for twenty
minutes. When you fall for somebody it really does
turn you into a prize idiot. But it feels so delicious,
you don't give a damn, anyway.

Chloe started to play a game of tag and tickling
with Toby and Ferg to prove that she hadn't got a
hangover. I wasn't in the mood for tag and I dread
tickling because, to me, tickling is the ultimate
torture. I start to feel trapped and hysterical as if I'm

going to faint or die. So I just went on walking by the waves and feeling kind of glamorous and deliciously alone like someone in a movie, and imagining how fabulous it would be if Beast was walking towards me.

Suddenly I realised that somebody was walking towards me, along the edge of the ocean, but it was Oliver. He was alone, too. Maybe he'd ditched Morgan big time, or maybe she'd just nipped into town to buy some extra, extra thick mascara to frame those gorgeous melting eyes. In some cheesy movie we would run in slow-motion towards each other and embrace in the surf, while the music of Beethoven or somebody throbbed away in the background.

But this wasn't a movie and that wasn't going to happen. Not if I had anything to do with it.

CHAPTER 38

I stood and stared out to sea with my beady little rodent's eyes, but I was kind of watching Oliver secretly, sideways, all the time he was coming towards me. I put my hands in my pockets to show how nonchalant I felt. My heart was thumping, but not in quite the same way as it used to. I wasn't scared in case I made a fool of myself. I was scared in case he made a fool of himself.

As we met he gave a sort of theatrical start, as if he hadn't seen me.

'Oh, hi, Zoe,' he said.

'You missed a good match,' I said.

He twitched in an odd kind of way. 'Rugby doesn't really do it for me, to be honest,' he drawled.

'Morgan is gorgeous!' I enthused, suddenly

changing the subject in another uncomfortable direction. Uncomfortable for him, that is. I felt weirdly, magnificently comfortable. I felt stronger with every second that passed. I had crossed some sort of divide between the old days when I was totally in his power, and the glorious present in which I suddenly felt I could say what I liked, and I didn't care what he thought. 'Where did you meet her?'

Oliver kind of winced and tilted his head on one side. 'At a party . . .' he said, pulling an unenthusiastic face as if he was describing his meeting with a rancid old dog. 'Her dad owns a hotel, well, a string of hotels, in fact . . .'

'Hey, terrific!' I was teasing him relentlessly now. 'You could inherit big time.' Oliver went a bit pale, and moved the sand about with his feet. I'd always thought his awkwardness was touching, but now I began to realise it might be all an act to avoid taking responsibility for anything.

'Oh no,' he said. 'It's just . . . uhh . . . you know . . . I'm not sure really how . . . You know, uh, weird things happen.' Then he gave me a strange look. A kind of anguished burning look as if to say, *Morgan grabbed me when I wasn't paying attention, otherwise I'd be at your side, you gorgeous pouting creature, Zoe Morris!*

I understood every tiny detail of his look: he was asking me to keep up the adoration without giving anything back. Just keeping his options open. But I wasn't having any! I stepped back slightly and gave him the most dazzling, ironical smile.

'Well, I think Morgan's just amazing!' I grinned. 'And I reckon you're a very lucky guy! She seems totally besotted with you.'

He must have known I was taking the piss, but he seemed lost for words. He plainly hadn't got used to the new, free, confident me – he was so expecting me to throw myself at his feet and lick his boots just like I always used to. Maybe he'd expected me to say, 'Morgan's a very lucky girl', not the other way round.

'Oh, I dunno . . .' He shrugged, and gave me a sly smile – a last try to winkle some ego-boosting drivel out of me. But I refused to oblige. I was actually quite shocked that he hadn't got the courtesy to accept compliments to his girlfriend, even if she was so clearly a demented slapper. He so should have said, 'Yes, I'm really lucky.' But instead all he could manage was a treacherous shrug.

I finally realised that despite the fact that he looked like a hero in a medieval fairy tale, he didn't have a gallant bone in his body. Last night, when

Chloe had sent out her cry for help, he'd just sat there in the cybercafe and let me go off on my own, into a goddam *fight* for goodness' sake! If anybody was a medieval knight around here, it was me!

'Well – gotta go – I'm visiting Tam in hospital in a min,' I said. Oliver kind of flinched.

'Oh yes! How is she? I heard she'd had her appendix out . . .'

'Yeah. It all happened last night, right after the fight behind the silver door. It was some evening. Crisis after crisis.' I gave him a hard look to indicate, *And you didn't lift a finger to help me.*

'Give her my – er, regards,' said Oliver. 'And say I hope she gets better soon.'

'Sure,' I replied. 'Catch you later, OK?' And I walked off. I have rarely felt so triumphant. I didn't look back.

I walked over to where Chloe and Toby and Ferg were still wrestling in an idle sort of way, as if they were running out of steam.

'So what did Oliver say?' hissed Tobe. 'Did he say, "I've ditched the slapper and I'll be yours till the end of time, Queen of my Heart"?'

'Yeah, something like that.' I grinned. 'And I told him he could take a running jump.'

'Really?' Chloe came up close and stared deep into my eyes.

'Oliver,' I announced, 'sucks.' There was an uncertain silence for a moment, and then they all cheered. 'The only mystery,' I added, 'is why it took me so long to realise what he was really like.'

'I never rated him,' said Toby. 'He kind of acts superior all the time.'

'He'sFromAnotherPlanet!' giggled Ferg.

'OK, no more about Oliver!' I insisted. 'Too boring!'

'Right,' said Toby, 'I'm going to spend the next couple of hours with a beautiful girl in bed.'

'What?' I gasped. But Tobe hadn't got unexpectedly lucky. It was his way of saying he wanted to visit Tam in hospital. 'It's just an excuse to buy some lilies and grapes.' He grinned.

I knew I'd be visiting Tam later, with my family, but I thought I'd send her a little message. I tore a page out of my notebook.

Hi, Tam! See you later. So sorry I didn't realise you had the big A. Hope you'll feel better soon. Loads and loads and loads of love, Z. xxx

I scribbled a little drawing of Tam in bed with a rabbit and a chick looking after her.

When Toby and Ferg had gone, Chloe and I strolled up and down the beach again. We couldn't get enough of it. The wind whipped our hair about and made our cheeks tingle.

'So you're over Oliver, and I think I'm over Brendan,' announced Chloe. 'I had a weird kind of depression after he went off to Edinburgh, but now I realise he was just a stupid flirt.'

'The fellow's a frightful cad,' I said in a 1940s film voice. We walked some more. The waves were crashing wonderfully. Surfers soared along then toppled into the foam. Chloe took my arm and squeezed it.

'Are you sure about Oliver, though?' she asked. 'Morgan's just a distraction; she's so obviously wrong for him. Toby reckons he's going to dump her by tomorrow.'

'I don't care if he never dumps her,' I told her. 'I realise now I've been going off him for ages. Every time I met him I felt kind of disappointed afterwards. I know he's good-looking, but he just kind of can't be bothered. I used to think he was divinely shy, but I realise now he's actually just lazy. And vain. He likes being adored. And he's always dissing other guys. Well, I've had it up to here with adoring. As far as

I'm concerned, I hope they stay an item for ever, and that she makes him cringe every half hour for the rest of his life.' I grinned.

'Harsh,' commented Chloe thoughtfully, 'but maybe he deserves it.'

'Yes,' I said. 'I wouldn't go out with him if he was the last man left alive.' The ironical echoes of this statement reverberated in my secret heart. If only Chloe knew how things had changed for me! Oliver was only half the story.

We walked along the beach some more, arm in arm. Eventually Beast and the guys appeared in clean togs and started playing some more beach games. My heart started to dance again. They waved. We waved back. But I just held on to Chloe's arm and we went on walking.

As Chloe and I strolled up and down, I thought about the last time I'd used that phrase about not ever fancying somebody if he was 'the last man alive'. It was only a few weeks since Beast had turned up out of the blue at my house, but it seemed like some freaky incident from a previous life. Beast fancying me and asking me out – and me getting in a rage and giving him several mouthfuls of abuse.

Now he seemed like a different person. What was

going on in his mind? The memory of what I'd said to him tormented me. I had misjudged him totally. I had believed the rumours about Beast without bothering to get to know the real Harry Hawkins. And as a result, we were finished before we'd even had a chance to begin.

Did he ever think about that night? Did he assume I still hated him? Did he hate me for rejecting him so rudely? I had to find out what he thought of me. I had to try and put things right, to let him know how my feelings had changed. Maybe there was the tiniest hint of a chance for me. But I wouldn't just need a brilliant strategy and a large slice of luck to turn things around. Frankly, I'd need a miracle.

CHAPTER 39

Having walked up and down the beach a dozen times, Chloe and I decided to revisit our childhood and make a sandcastle. It was very stylish, but we disagreed about turrets. Basically Chloe wanted a fairytale sandcastle with lots of shells and pinnacles and I wanted a minimalist sandcastle with very smooth everything. We do vaguely plan to share a flat somewhere, one day, when we've finished our education, but I have a feeling it could cause a few rows.

Some time later my mum and dad appeared. They were arm in arm. My mum's cheeks had gone pink in the wind, and she was wearing a French sailor-type outfit of white culottes and a stripy T-shirt. Dad was wearing shorts. Thank God they reached down to his knees, and were a plain cream colour. Mum tries to keep a tight rein on his mad clothes sense.

'We couldn't sleep much,' said Mum. 'It's going to be better if we have a little nap this afternoon. My body clock's all wrong because of driving down through the night.'

'How's Tam?' I asked. 'What's the latest?'

'She's fine,' said Dad. 'She sent us a text. We're going to see her later. She'll be turning cartwheels again by tomorrow.'

Just then Beast and his team came jogging up. My heart gave a frenzied throb. I felt ridiculously nervous. He grinned at us, looking as if he was planning to run on by.

'Oh!' I spluttered, 'That's Beast Hawkins – the guy who called the ambulance!'

'We must thank him,' cried Mum eagerly.

'Beast!' I called. He came over. The rest of the guys jogged on. 'Beast, uh . . . Harry,' I said, blushing, 'this is my mum and dad. They want to thank you for what you did yesterday.'

'Hello there!' said Beast, extending a hand to Mum and then to Dad. 'I didn't do anything. It was Zoe who told me Tam had a tummy ache.'

'But you realised what was happening! You called

the ambulance and everything!' gushed Mum. 'And you went with Tam to the hospital! That was so important!'

'Honestly, anyone would have done the same,' said Beast, looking embarrassed.

'I'm going to give them merry hell at our local hospital back home about this,' said Mum, seething. 'Poor Tam had such a bad pain we had to call an ambulance, only a few weeks ago! She spent a night in there under observation! And they missed it completely!'

'I think a grumbling appendix can be kind of hard to diagnose, sometimes,' said Beast thoughtfully. 'How is she now?'

'Recovering,' said Dad. 'We're going to visit her again at lunchtime.'

'It must have been a bit of a nightmare,' said Beast. 'The drive down and everything.'

'Oh, awful!' agreed Mum. 'I've never been so terrified in my life! She could have died!'

'But you told me nobody ever died of appendicitis,' I gasped, staring at Beast. He gave me a strange, awkward smile.

'I didn't want to worry you, Zoe,' he said. 'You had enough on your plate.'

'Anyway,' said Dad cheerily, 'she's going to be fine!'

'Are you planning to stay around for a few days?' asked Beast.

'Yes!' said Mum. 'We've found a lovely flat up there!' She pointed to the distant cliffs where Blue Ocean Flats were visible with their sparkling white walls and blue-painted window frames.

'Awesome!' commented Beast. 'Must have great views!'

'You must come up and have lunch with us one day or something.' said Mum. 'How about tomorrow? There's a wonderful balcony.'

'If you can spare the time,' added Dad, 'from your busy schedule saving lives.'

'Oh, I'm sorry, but I'm leaving today,' said Beast regretfully. 'I have to get back home. I start work again tomorrow morning.'

A horrid little squeeze of disappointment passed through my insides. Beast was leaving today! And I wouldn't see him again for ages.

'What a shame,' said Mum. 'Oh well, have a good journey home.'

'Thanks,' said Beast with a courteous smile. 'I hope Tam gets better soon.' He didn't look at me at all. 'It's been a pleasure meeting you.'

'Thanks again for what you did,' repeated Mum. 'I don't think we'll ever be able to repay you.'

Beast backed off, smiling and putting up his hands to fend off any more gratitude. Then suddenly, for a split second, he looked at me. It pierced my heart.

'Bye, Zoe,' he said. 'See you later.' Then he jogged off.

'What a charming young man,' said Mum as we resumed our walk. 'Such lovely manners! What's his name again?'

'Harry,' I said. It sounded glamorous somehow.

'Hmmm,' added Dad, 'he's going to be a doctor, you said? Don't let Mum get hold of his telephone number – she'll be pestering him day and night about her aches and pains.'

They started laughing together about Mum's hypochondria. Suddenly I recognised Oliver and Morgan walking towards us. They waved and walked on.

'Who was that?' asked Mum.

'Oliver Wyatt and his girlfriend,' I told her. 'You know, he worked at the farm with us.'

'Wasn't he a heart-throb of yours once, Zoe?'

asked Dad. His memory can be inconveniently sharp sometimes.

'Oh no, Dad,' I said. 'That was a different Oliver.'

After a while my parents went back to the flat to try and have another sleep. We promised to join them later and maybe visit Tam. But right now, Chloe and I wanted a little bit more sea and surf. We didn't talk much. We just sat on the beach and stared at the waves.

'Everything's sorted now, isn't it?' mused Chloe happily. I was drawing circles in the sand. 'We're going to have a terrific time.' I nodded. 'You know we were saying that we're independent now and we don't need boys in our lives and they just mess everything up?' Chloe went on. 'Well, we're still allowed to fancy them, aren't we?' She grinned impishly. 'Because I tell you what – I'd give Dave Cheng eight out of ten for sex appeal, wouldn't you?'

'Possibly,' I replied evasively. I wasn't thinking of Dave Cheng.

'Just wait till you get over Oliver,' said Chloe. 'I bet you'll fall for some new guy by the end of the week.' I gave a kind of disbelieving smile, but it felt thin and false.

'I don't think so,' I said.

Chloe threw herself back on to the sand and looked up at the sky. She gave a huge contented sigh.

'Isn't it absolutely brilliant being here?' she said. 'And everything's sorted, isn't it?'

'Yeah,' I agreed. Though to be honest, things seemed less sorted than they had ever been.

If only I'd known two months ago what I knew now: that Oliver was a waste of time, and Beast was some kind of superhero. But I'd had my chance with Beast, and I'd blown it. How could I have rejected him in that foul way? If only I'd known then how adorable he really was!

But might I have a chance with him, even at this late stage? Would Chloe buy it or would she be mysteriously furious? There was maybe just the tiniest chance . . . but I was going to have to transform myself utterly if any green shoots of love were to germinate.

'Chloe . . . ?' I ventured, 'how about a nice little new project? I think I might try and reinvent myself, like, to be totally charismatic and stylish and grand. Unrecognisable, in fact.'

Chloe grinned. She looked interested. 'Let's go for it!' she agreed. 'Girls to goddesses in seven days . . .' I wasn't sure it could be done in seven days. I wasn't sure it could be done at all. But it was my last little shred of hope, and I was clinging to it. Girls to goddesses! Why not?